FIRE
IN THE
HOLE!

BY
MARY CRONK FARRELL

CLARION BOOKS

NEW YORK

To Brandon,
As you strike out on your own

Clarion Books
a Houghton Mifflin Company imprint
215 Park Avenue South, New York, NY 10003
Copyright © 2004 by Mary Cronk Farrell

The type was set in 12-point Aldus Roman.

www.houghtonmifflinbooks.com

Printed in the U.S.A.

Library of Congress Cataloging-in-Publication Data
Farrell, Mary Cronk.
Fire in the hole! / by Mary Cronk Farrell.
p. cm.
Summary: A claustrophobic boy dreams of going to college and becoming a
newspaperman rather than a miner like his father, but when all union miners
in the Coeur d'Alene Mining District are arrested, Mick develops new respect
for his father while taking over responsibility for his family.
ISBN 0-618-44634-6
[1. Lead mines and mining—Fiction. 2. Fathers and sons—Fiction. 3. Family
life—Idaho—Fiction. 4. Labor unions—Fiction. 5. Self-actualization
(Psychology)—Fiction. 6. Coeur d'Alene Mining District (Idaho)—Fiction.
7. Idaho—History—20th century—Fiction.] I. Title.
PZ7.F246113Fi 2004
[Fic]—dc22   2004004501

ISBN-13: 978-0-618-44634-6
ISBN-10: 0-618-44634-6

MV 10 9 8 7 6 5 4 3 2 1

ACKNOWLEDGMENTS

I could not have written this book without the many people who have supported and encouraged me. I would especially like to thank my friends and family, and also those who so generously shared time and expertise to assist me in the research for this novel: John Fahey, historian and author; John Amonson of the Wallace District Mining Museum, Wallace, Idaho; Elbert and Laura Pillars of the Boomerang Printing Museum, Palouse, Washington; Bill Lane, owner of the Crystal Gold Mine, Kellogg, Idaho; Ray Chapman, former public relations executive for the Bunker Hill and Sullivan Mining Company; Katherine G. Aiken, professor of history at the University of Idaho; and Adam Raley and Lori Fontana for their help with Latin and Irish prayers. I'm grateful to those who read early drafts of the manuscript: Doris Farrell, Helen Farrell, Eric Akins, and Karlene Arguinchona. I deeply appreciate the Silver Valley hospitality of Steve Gilseth at Ace Lock & Key, Osburn, Idaho, who promptly, graciously, and at no charge responded to my call for help when I locked my keys in my car while on a research trip.

I would also like to thank Jan, Angela, Lorraine, Phyllis, Maurie, Jennifer, and Cherry, who were there for me at the click of a mouse as I took my baby steps in writing for children. I gained much from their constant encouragement and willingness to share their knowledge.

I am deeply grateful for the friendship, generosity, skill, wisdom, and support of my writing group: Meghan Nuttall Sayres, Claire Rudolf Murphy, Mary Douthitt, and Lynn Caruso.

I am most grateful to my husband, Mike, for his love and trust, and for his support, both emotional and financial, and to my editor, Virginia Buckley, who gave Mick's story life as a book.

WARDNER, IDAHO, 1899

ONE

*C*lomp. *Clomp-clomp.* Mick Shea jumped to his feet at the sound of his father on the stoop. *Clomp. Clomp-clomp.* The familiar stomp as Da knocked the mud off his miner's boots set Mick's nerves atingle. But it was too late.

He had no time to hide the book. Da came through the door and crossed the room in two strides. The dank, metallic smell of the mine swirled around him, seeping from his pores. Blinking against the gray dust billowing from Da's hair and clothing, Mick backed away. The three-legged stool on which he'd been perched fell into the corner behind the wood stove.

A rasping cough stopped Da short. He fought to clear his lungs, to get air. Frozen by the rage that showed through the grime on Da's face, Mick gripped the book to his chest.

Catching his breath, Da tore the book from Mick's hands. Using the tail of his shirt, he yanked open the stove door and pitched the book in. It settled into the flames with a *floosh.*

"No!" Mick tried to push past his father and reach into the stove, but Da was a head taller and well muscled from his work in the mines. Mick could only watch, clenching his fists. The fire licked around the pages, as though tasting the edge of each, then consumed the book in a burst of blue and orange.

"The woodbin is empty and you sit there like a king with nothing to do."

Mick cringed at the disgust thick in Da's voice.

"Michael . . ." Mam begged her husband from the adjoining bedroom. "Leave the boy be."

Mick raised his chin and stared straight into his father's furious eyes. "You've no right to burn that book," he said.

He saw the punch coming, braced himself, didn't flinch. The force of the blow snapped his head back and slammed his teeth together. He cried out. He couldn't help it. Dizzy with pain, he stumbled across the kitchen to the back door.

"You want to eat, you work like the rest of us. You could shoot a rabbit or two and skin 'em, bring in the wood and fill the water pail. Your mam needin' help and you sittin' on your arse . . ."

Mick went out, shutting the door on Da's words. He held his stomach with both hands. He wouldn't throw up. He wouldn't.

Mr. Delaney had lent Mick the book *Oliver Twist*. How would he replace it? Or learn if Oliver ever found a real home?

He should have known Da would be coming home. But the details of Oliver's life in the orphanage seemed to have leapt off the page and become so real that Mick had forgotten to listen for his father's footsteps.

He groaned, frustration adding to the pain. Opening his eyes, he took a few steps in the deepening twilight. The horizon tilted, but he made it to behind the woodpile before his insides took over and heaved up the whole sour lot of it.

"Micky."

He straightened up to see his sister, Bridey.

"Here. . . . Let me." She held a wet cloth. He took it, spit bile on the ground, and wiped his lips and chin.

"I hate him," Mick snarled under his breath.

"He's not himself." Bridey wrung her hands. "You know . . . since things started getting worse at the mine."

"Oh, he's himself, all right." Mick turned his back on his sister and started picking up a load of wood. The labor union meetings did seem to stir up Da, but it was more than that.

"He's just plain mean." Mick didn't try to hold back his bitterness.

"Micky . . ." Bridey tugged at his sleeve. "Try not to cross him. I—I can't bear—"

"Hey." He swung around. "Yell 'Fire in the hole!' or something to let me know when Da's coming." Everyone in a mining town knew the warning shout. "Fire in the hole!" signaled that the fuse was lit and the dynamite was ready to blow.

Bridey stepped back. "I—I didn't know he was in one of his moods," she said. A single tear made a track down her cheek. Now Mick felt guilty.

"It's nothing." He made his voice light and tried to grin, but the effort sent a zinger through his jawbone. He turned away to pick up the ax, then swung around to his sister again.

"Don't worry about me," he said. "I know what I'm doing. He won't stop me."

The back door opened, and the light of a lantern bobbed

across the ground. Mick picked up another piece of fire-wood; his back tensed, as he waited for Da's angry voice to ring out. But it was Mam who called to him.

"Mick," she said. "Please go to the cellar and bring up potatoes for supper."

"Yes'm." He dropped the wood and took the lantern. Though he feared another rage from Da, he would sooner have returned to the house than go down into the dark, damp depths of the ground.

He heaved open the plank door, revealing blackness below. The lantern cast a golden circle on the steps, and he started down. It was like descending into a mineshaft. The creak of timbers, the smell of earth—Mick shuddered. A cold sweat sprang out on his upper lip.

The cellar was deep enough that he could stand to his full height, but the earthen walls and board ceiling, which he knew was covered with dirt and sod, seemed to press in upon him. It didn't matter how many times he came down here, how many times he told himself there was no danger. The terror of being buried alive always swept over him.

Trying not to think, Mick set down the lantern and started to fill his shirt with potatoes from the bin. Only small ones with sprouting eyes seemed to be left. Inhaling in quick little gasps, his head light, he fought the urge to run back up the stairs. He tossed two rotten potatoes out the door before he found enough to fill the soup pot and escape.

Gulping fresh air, Mick dropped the cellar door closed and hurried to the house. He paused outside the kitchen, listening. All was quiet. Da must have used up his temper. As he went in, he blew out the lantern, then spilled the potatoes onto the drainboard and glanced around. Bridey stood at the wood stove minding a simmering pot. His eight-year-old brother, Nat, sat at the table working sums.

"Mam's resting a bit before supper," Bridey said, not turning from her stirring. "Da's with her."

Since Mam was in her ninth month, it was not unusual for her to lie down in the late afternoon, but the set of his sister's back told Mick that Bridey was worried. Mam had lost two babies, both stillborn, in the years between Bridey and Nat.

Mick was relieved later when Mam appeared in time for the evening meal. Da held out her chair at one end of the table, and she sank into it.

Nobody spoke. Bridey passed around thick slices of the graham bread she had made that day and then ladled out the soft chunks of potato in broth.

Mick mashed his potato against the side of his bowl. His jaw hurt too much to chew. He scowled at Nat, who had the manners of a puppy. The boy had slurped down his soup and was now holding his bowl up for more. Mick kicked him under the table.

"Ow!" Nat clipped off his yelp as Bridey shushed him with a finger to her lips.

"More, Da?" she asked.

"Half a bowl. Give the rest to Mick. Lad, you gonna make it in the mines, you need some beef on your bones."

Mick tightened his grip on his spoon. He shook his head at Bridey, avoiding Da's look.

"Ah, give it to me, then, Bridey, my girl." Da chuckled. Holding up his bowl, he threw a broad wink at Bridey.

Mick gritted his teeth. Da was good at that. Dropping his anger like a dirty shirt and turning on the charm. His father might choose to forget what had happened before supper, but that didn't mean Mick would.

He glanced at Mam at the end of the gingham-covered table. She smiled at him, but he saw a certain strain at the corners of her mouth. Her face was pale and surrounded by the same black curls he saw tumbling into his own eyes whenever he glimpsed himself in the water pail. Bridey and Nat had Da's hair, the reddish gold color of straw in the late-afternoon sun.

"I got beef on *my* bones," Nat said. "I wanna be a nipper. Jimmy's a nipper, and he's not even as strong as me."

"Jimmy's da is a dirty rotten scab," said Da. "You stay away from—*Aaugh! Aaugh! Aaugh!*" Da waved a hand at Nat and gave in to a fit of miner's consumption.

Each time Da fought to fill his scarred lungs with air, Mick almost couldn't breathe himself. His father had bragged for years that he was too tough to be hurt by a little mine dust. But when the miners started using the new machine drills, there had been more than a little dust. Mick had watched Da begin to suffer the shortness of breath and wracking cough that eventually weakened and even killed men.

Mam had dropped her spoon and was watching Da, a crease across her forehead. Then she turned a stern eye on Nat. "You'll finish school before you go to work in any mine," she said.

Da slammed a closed hand on the table, rattling the tin bowls. Mick lowered his head and kept eating. "Burbidge brought in a dozen more scabs from Missouri today," Da said. "The Bunker Hill's the only mine in the district won't pay union wages. Hiring scabs . . ." Da marked each word with a sharp thrust of his spoon in the air. "Burbidge'll run all us union miners out by summer."

"Burbidge should hang," said Nat. He copied Da, balling his fingers and hitting the table.

"Nat!" Mam spoke sharply. "I'll have no talk of violence at this table."

"But that's what they're all saying at the union hall," Nat replied.

Mam held up a finger to silence him, and she seemed to want to do the same to Da. But she knew better. Mick met Bridey's eyes across the table, then looked into his empty bowl.

"The good Lord will smite 'em down," Da continued. "He'll use the union to do it. We'll beat Burbidge and the whole Bunker Hill and Sullivan Company."

"Michael . . ." Mam stood and walked over to Da. Stopping behind him, she wrapped her arms around his shoulders. "The good Lord will smite you with indigestion."

Da's angry face softened as he took hold of Mam's hands. "The company can't keep us trampled forever—not when we got the prettiest women you ever laid eyes on." He smiled up at her.

"Hope you haven't forgotten tomorrow night, Michael," Mam said, kissing the top of his head. "We could do with a little comedy."

Da laughed and raised Mam's work-roughened fingers to his lips. "Moira, I promised I'd take you to the show," he said. "And I'm a man of my word."

7

Mick again traded a glance with his sister. This time the tightness in his chest gave way a bit, but he couldn't help his eyes darting to the stove. Exploring the bruise on his chin with a fingertip, he wondered how he could tell Mr. Delaney what had happened to the book.

TWO

As he entered the office of the *Wardner Bugle* after school the next day, Mick pulled the sharp scent of ink into his lungs. It smelled a bit like the shoe polish Da rubbed into his worn brogans on Sunday mornings, but stronger, thicker, somehow promising. Mick imagined the ink—the words on the newsprint—as alive and powerful.

But today the newspaper office didn't enliven his spirits. His stomach was a lump of dread. Mr. Delaney was sure to ask him about the book.

The editor sat on an oak stool in front of the type case, a shoulder-high wood chest with a dozen drawers full of foundry type. Each letter, each punctuation mark, was molded from lead and stuck on a tiny block of wood. With a pair of tweezers, the newsman picked up letters one by one and set type on the composing stick, a piece of wood that held one line at a time. When complete, each line of type was carefully transferred to a tin tray, a galley, eventually making a paragraph, and then an entire column of paragraphs.

When Mick came in, Mr. Delaney stood and stretched his arms over his head, flexing his fingers. "That's quite a bruise, Master Shea. Get in a schoolyard fight?"

Mick licked his lips, turned away, and began gathering loose type from the top of the case and putting it back into the proper drawer.

"I respect a man who stands up for his principles, but violence usually doesn't solve anything."

Mick squirmed under Mr. Delaney's gaze. "It wasn't a fight." He could see that the editor didn't believe him. "I— I ran into a—a tree branch."

"Oh." The editor returned to his stool and picked up his tweezers. "Your da pretty sore about Bunker Hill refusing to pay union scale?"

"He's riled good," said Mick, relieved that Mr. Delaney had let up about his black-and-blue cheek.

"I'm afraid there's going to be more trouble before this is over," said Mr. Delaney.

"What do you mean?"

"Look here." The editor pointed to the stone, a high table topped with a slab of flat, smooth stone. "It's all there on the front page."

On the stone, Mick saw three-quarters of the front page of the newspaper laid out inside an iron frame called a chase. After a column was completed in the galley, it was transferred to the chase.

"STRIKE!!" The headline spread across the middle columns of type. Reading it was like looking at a mirror image of the newspaper. It had been strange and difficult for Mick when he was first helping out at the newspaper office a year ago. But now he could read backward nearly as fast as he could forward. Below the headline, in slightly smaller type, he read:

VIOLENCE THREATENED

WARDNER, Idaho, April 27—The Western Federation of Miners voted last night to strike the Bunker Hill. Union Secretary Jack Hocking accuses the Bunker Hill and Sullivan Mining Company of firing local union miners and recruiting non-union labor from out of state to work at lower wages.

A union source says members have guns and will use them if necessary to protect their jobs.

The Bunker Hill remains the only operation in the Coeur d'Alene District steadfastly refusing to pay underground workers union scale of $3.50 a day. Company officials do not recognize the union and say they will not meet with representatives.

Mick read the article twice. Then crossing the room to yank on Mr. Delaney's elbow he asked, "What's going to happen? Will there be a fight between the union and the scabs?"

"Hold on. Let me finish this."

Mick bit back more questions and watched the editor. He had finished a column in the galley and was now proofreading it, correcting misspellings and punctuation errors.

"There." Mr. Delaney laid down his tweezers. "You've heard the rumor that the union's been stockpiling guns?"

"Yes. But nobody wants a fight, do they?"

The editor sighed and interlocked his slender fingers, turning his palms out and extending his arms. Mick heard his knuckles crack.

"People are bound to get killed if they bring out guns," said Mick.

"You're right, and most of the union men would agree with you. But it only takes a few hotheads. . . ." Mr. Delaney shook his head. He put a hand on Mick's shoulder, but his thoughts seemed far away. Did the talk of violence scare him, too? "Ready to lock up the chase, Mick?"

Glad to think about something else, Mick took the column that Mr. Delaney had just completed and carried it to the stone. But his hands were shaking, and as he slid the finished column off the galley and into the chase, the last line of type fell to the floor. Bending over to pick up the loose pieces of type, he knocked the chase with his elbow. The frame holding the front page of the next morning's edition of the *Wardner Bugle* slid to the edge of the stone. There was a sound like the scattering of cracked corn on a hen house floor.

The bottom corner of the frame had slid off the stone, and part of a column—hundreds of letters, spacers, and punctuation—had fallen out, scattered like pages turned to bits of ash.

"I'm sorry—" Mick fell to his knees, scrambling after the tiny letters. "I'll fix it. Don't worry." Throwing a quick glance at Mr. Delaney, he scooped up handfuls and then attacked the mess of type, trying to make words from the jumble. He jumped when he felt a hand on his shoulder.

"Take it easy," said the editor. "We'll work on this together."

"That was clumsy," said Mick.

"Everybody makes mistakes. Settle down."

Mr. Delaney handed Mick the tweezers. He dictated sentences, and Mick picked through the letters and assembled the words. Together they rebuilt the column. It felt good, as if he and the editor were partners.

Mr. Delaney's words broke into Mick's thoughts. "I do sympathize with the union men. Mine owners don't much care about the lives of the workers. They're out to make a profit, pure and simple." He wiped his hands on his pants, which were already smeared with ink. "Lock it up?"

"Sure." Mick snugged the chase by adding the blocks of wood known as spacers. The type had to be packed tightly so it wouldn't fall out when he picked up the iron frame and carried it to the flatbed printing press.

The press was the heart of the newspaper. It stood at the back of the office and took up half the room. The editor flipped the electric switch and the flatbed began to thrust forward and back. The huge cylinder started to turn, inking the pages, and the whole building shook.

Mick liked to stay until he and Mr. Delaney had put the paper to bed, but after Da's fit of temper the night before, he decided to head home early. "Gotta go." He shouted to be heard over the clanging of the press. "Chores." He mimed chopping wood.

Mr. Delaney grunted and nodded as he continued to feed pages of newsprint into the printing press. But he mouthed something at Mick.

"What?" Mick stepped closer.

". . . *Oliver Twist?*"

With news of the strike, Mick had forgotten all about the book.

Mr. Delaney grinned. "Don't worry," he said. "Take all

13

the time you want. I think you'll enjoy it once you get started."

"It's not that. I do like it. I mean, I did like it."

Mr. Delaney raised an eyebrow.

"I . . . I lost the book," said Mick. He pushed hair off his sweaty forehead. He couldn't meet Mr. Delaney's eyes.

"Lost it?"

"I must have dropped it . . . or . . . or something."

Mr. Delaney fed another page into the press, then squinted at him.

Mick swallowed. "I'm sorry." He forced the words out above the noise of the press. Then he turned and fled, cursing himself as he ran home. Mr. Delaney had more books than anyone in town, probably more than anyone in the Coeur d'Alenes. Mick had been so happy when Mr. Delaney suggested he borrow any one he wanted to read. That would probably never happen again.

Mick went straight to the woodshed. Eyeing the stacked wood, he chose a large chunk and carried it to the chopping block. Stepping back, he raised the ax over his head.
Thwaack!

Da had no right to burn that book.
Thwaack!

No right to hit him.
Thwaack!

Again and again he attacked, every stroke hitting home. He didn't hear Da's footsteps.

THREE

When the last wedge of log fell away, Mick put down the ax and looked up. There stood his father. He had no idea how long Da had been watching him. He fell back a step and licked his lips.

The shriek of a steam whistle sounded in the distance, along with the constant *thump-ump-ump* of the mills crushing rock, separating and concentrating minerals. The noise never stopped in a hard-rock mining town.

Wardner sat perched in a gulch formed by the steep sides of two hills rich with galena, a shiny gray ore containing mostly lead and some silver. The mining companies made profit enough from the lead and tiny veins of silver to keep digging in hopes of finding a mother lode. Tunnels sunk deep under the town pulsed with dynamite explosions that loosened the ore and sent constant rumblings through the streets. Dust from the blasts and smoke from the mills belched into the air day and night. The chugging of steam engines added to a clamor so familiar that Mick usually didn't notice it.

Now as he stared at his father's boots, he feared that his beating heart sounded loudest of all.

"Mick." Da spoke quietly, and Mick looked up.

15

"I—I'm sorry about the book." His father put his hands in his trousers pockets and then took them out again. "I was wrong to burn it." Da nudged a wood chip back and forth with the toe of his boot.

"It was Mr. De—"

"But you shouldn't be wasting your time reading. You should be helping more. Your mam's not feeling well these days."

Mick turned on his heel and walked away. Da wasn't sorry at all. He grabbed another log from the woodpile. Small and dry, good for kindling. Putting it on the chopping block, he picked up the ax. Da had remained standing there. He was saying something, but Mick started splitting the wood, ignoring him.

". . . Shakespeare."

Mick stopped with the ax in midair. He looked at Da and saw a wide smile on his face.

"What did you say?" asked Mick.

"I said, your mam isn't up to going out tonight. Would you like to go see the show? It's a traveling Shakespeare company."

Mick lowered the ax. *Yes,* his mind shouted. But the words wouldn't come out. How dare his father act as though everything was all right? Throw a book in the fire one day, be all smiling and nice the next. He turned his back and began to stack the wood he'd cut. He heard the door shut as Da went inside.

When Mick went in later, Mam met him at the door. "Better hurry and clean up," she said. "The play starts at seven."

"I'm not going."

"You're mad at your da." She raised an eyebrow at him. "Don't chop off your nose to spite your face."

"But this was supposed to be *your* night out, Mam." Mick looked down at his hands and, noticing a hangnail, began to pick at it. "It's not my place to go."

"If *he* don't wanna go, I will." Nat thrust himself between them. "Please, Mam, can I go?"

Mam gathered her youngest into a hug and tried to smooth his mussed hair. "You'll get your chance, Nat."

Meeting Mick's eyes over his brother's head, she said, "Mick, I want this for you. Please?"

He couldn't refuse his mother, even if he had wanted to. "I'll go," he said.

After a quick supper, Mick and Da, dressed in their Sunday best, walked downtown. Mick could hear the brass band and loud laughter before they reached the Grand Theater. The double doors were propped open to the street, and sounds spilled out as fast as the crowd surged in.

"Hope we get a seat," said Da. "Shakespeare pulls a different crowd than the usual burlesque show." He laughed and handed their tickets to a thin man in a striped suit who was standing just inside the doors and who directed them to the right.

The crowd stood so thick that they couldn't do more than shuffle through the lobby. Stretched up on tiptoe, Mick tried to see everything at once. Shining electric globes lit the room as if it were broad day. Men dressed in suits and women in full skirts and feathered hats pressed forward, calling to one another over the music. Some climbed an

17

open stair to the upper level, but Mick followed Da's square shoulders though a side door that led to the main floor of the theater.

A blood-red curtain hid the stage, and just in front of the stage sat the band, playing a march so lively it set Mick's head nodding. Comfortable-looking seats took up the center of the room, with rows of pine benches filling either side.

"Side seats," said Da, turning back to Mick and gesturing toward the benches. Those closest to the front were filled, but they found an empty spot halfway along the aisle.

As Mick sat down, a handkerchief fluttered down through the air in front of him. He looked up at the boxes, which were draped with bunting and tassels, and recognized Mr. Burbidge, manager of the Bunker Hill mine. With him sat a woman, her neck glittering with diamonds. As Mick watched, they were joined by several other couples and by a single man he recognized as Godfrey Snipes. Snipes was the only one who looked as though he didn't belong. His suit lacked the impeccable cut of those of the other men, and rather than an air of confidence, Snipes gave off the air of a bootlick. Mick had heard how the man hadn't lasted his first day in the mines and had instead wormed his way into employment as Burbidge's assistant. The fine clothes and elegant style of the others in the box held Mick's attention until a movement in the rafters drew his gaze.

Boards had been laid between the joists far overhead to make room for the overflow crowd. Legs dangled as men with worn work shoes settled themselves for the show. Mick felt dizzy just seeing them up there and lowered his eyes as the music stopped and the lights went out.

With slow jerks, the curtain was drawn aside on the opening scene of *A Midsummer Night's Dream.*

The play began with Egeus dragging his daughter, Hermia, before Theseus, Duke of Athens. He demanded that the duke force Hermia to marry the man he had chosen for her, Demetrius.

THESEUS: What say you, Hermia? Be advised, fair maid, To you your father should be as a god.
HERMIA: I would my father looked but with my eyes.
THESEUS: Rather your eyes must with his judgment look.

Mick concentrated, wanting to understand every word of the strange English. He leaned forward as the duke ordered Hermia to obey her father, or she'd be sent to a convent or killed. She decided to run away with her true love, Lysander.

Mick joined the rowdy audience clapping and cheering as the lovers escaped into the woods. He laughed as he had not in a long time when Puck enchanted the queen of the fairies, making her fall in love with a donkey.

When the curtain closed for intermission, Mick and Da stood with the others to stretch.

"Mighty fine show," said his father, grinning at him. He cupped his hands and spoke into Mick's ear to be heard over the sound of the band music. "Aren't you glad you came?"

Mick nodded.

"Shea . . ." The voice of Da's friend Joe Albinola floated over the crowd.

Mick turned to see Albinola coming down the aisle with John Kerr, the attorney who represented the union. Four or five miners followed them. Mick felt a stab of apprehension when he saw the grave expression on Albinola's face.

Albinola was a small man with a huge curly black beard and not a single hair on his shiny head. Mick liked his ready smile, the way his hands were always moving with his talk. But tonight he seemed different. Quieter, but sort of poised to spring.

"Did you hear about the explosion in the south crosscut tunnel?" Albinola asked.

Mick felt Da stiffen.

"Harriman's dead," said Albinola. "Doyle lost a leg."

Mick's father swore.

Harriman, thought Mick. *Petey's da? No, it couldn't be.*

Albinola turned and scowled up at the company men in the box. At that moment, the band ended its piece with a trumpet trill, and quiet filled the theater just as Albinola's voice rang out. "Industrialist pikers—one more dead miner means nothing to them."

The hush in the theater deepened. Mick stared at his father's friend and then at Burbidge up in the box. The company man rose to his feet.

"A tragedy, that explosion," he said, clearly meaning for his voice to carry down to the miners. "But the mine superintendent assures me the company bears no fault in the matter."

Albinola raised a fist. "Harriman leaves a wife and children. What's his family to do now?" he shouted.

Snipes had also risen to his feet. "Perhaps," he said,

projecting his voice across the theater, "a man with a wife and children should not have been so careless in his work."

Burbidge frowned and placed a hand on Snipes's shoulder, guiding him to sit down. "I regret the man's death," he said. "It's truly . . . a misfortune."

Mick looked from the men in the box to Albinola's blazing eyes and then to his father's face. The muscles of Da's neck stood out in rigid cords, and his eyes narrowed.

"Easy, Joe." Kerr, the attorney, stepped forward and took Albinola by the elbow. Jeers rained down from the men seated in the rafters, and Burbidge and his party started to look nervous. Then, with a roll on the drum, the band kicked off a rollicking two-step. It quickly drowned the commotion that had begun to rise from the miners, who made up most of the audience.

Albinola shook his fist one more time at the box overhead. Then he, Kerr, and Da bent their heads together in conversation. Mick tried to hear them over the sound of the music, but he couldn't. He stretched again and watched as groups of two and three miners who had gone out for fresh air returned to their seats.

He looked for Mr. Delaney but didn't see him. What he did notice was a dark flannel hat that was being passed from hand to hand in the rows of benches behind him. A flurry of hands digging into pockets and a certain somber ceremony moved the hat forward. What was this? Mick watched, but not until the hat neared him and he heard the whispers coming along with it did he understand.

"For Harriman's widow . . ."

". . . loyal union man."

"Help take care of Harriman's wee lads."

Mick felt the weight of coins as the hat came into his hands, and he stared at the crumpled paper money on top. Next to him, Da was opening the leather pouch he wore next to his skin. It bulged a little from the month's pay he had received earlier in the week. Without bothering to count the bills, Da shoved most of them into the hat and passed it on. Mick's mouth fell open, and he blinked at the thin, limp purse his father tucked back inside his clothes. Most of Da's pay went for rent and provisions. Rarely was there any money left over. It was good of Da to be so generous, but how would they make it until next payday?

The lights dimmed and the curtain opened. But Petey's father's face kept coming before Mick's eyes. Petey was Nat's age. Just a boy. What would it be like to never see your da alive again?

Mick looked sideways at his own father. Da's profile was strong in the dim light. Sometimes Mick hated him. The thought made him feel guilty. He wanted to forgive Da, to forget the times he was mean, but part of him wouldn't let go of his anger, didn't want to let go. Turning a shoulder to his father, he shut out all but the actors onstage, savoring Shakespeare's poetry like a rare treat of horehound candy.

When the play ended, Da huddled with Albinola and some of the union leadership while Mick stood apart. "We're going to the union hall," Da said after a moment. "Want to come along?"

"Got school in the morning," said Mick. "Better hit the sack."

The union headquarters was like a social club. Miners

gathered there to talk strategy against the mine owners, finishing off plenty of whiskey in the process, sometimes even fighting among themselves. Lots of boys, even those younger than Mick, liked to hang about. He didn't, especially not tonight.

Da shrugged. "Too good for the likes of us, huh?"

"No, Da. I—I just . . ."

But his father had walked away.

FOUR

The thin light of dawn was sifting into the loft when Mick opened his eyes the next morning. A sound had wakened him, the slightest of creaks—a door closing? He lay for a moment enjoying his warm bed, knowing he'd feel the cold floor on his bare feet soon enough. A piece of straw, poking up through the ticking, chafed at his skin, and he rolled over. Then he shot straight up. The spot beside him was empty. Nat was gone.

He kicked aside the wool blanket and pulled his pants and shirt on over the long johns he wore six months of the year. He went down the ladder as if it were a chute. Sure enough, Nat's shoes were missing from the rug by the door. Da's, too.

Outside, Mick paused in the mist that filled the narrow canyon. The sun hadn't yet risen above the Coeur d'Alene mountains, the forest-covered peaks surrounding the town that gave the area its name. A pair of crows called back and forth in the dim hint of dawn. Could it be the same pair he remembered from the year before? Crows mated for life, he'd learned, and their offspring didn't leave home but stayed around helping to raise the younger hatchlings. One big happy family. Mick snorted and headed for the center of town.

Rounding the corner by the Holley, Mason & Marks Company Hardware on Main Street, he saw in the half-light a group of miners heading down the gulch. It was a short distance to the flats where the railroad ran along the river. A lone figure trailed behind the miners. It was Nat. Mick ran after him. As he got closer, he could see that the men carried guns—Winchesters and Springfield rifles. He shivered.

"Hey, Nat!" Mick shouted, closing in on his brother when the ground leveled out near the Bunker Hill's ore concentrator, a gigantic building covered with red sheet iron. The first newspaper article he'd written all on his own for the *Bugle* had been about the concentrator. He smiled to himself remembering it.

BUNKER HILL
RESTARTS CONCENTRATOR

WARDNER, Idaho, Sept. 12—The Bunker Hill and Sullivan Mining Company today restarted its concentrator after a two-day shutdown for repairs. Manager Frederick Burbidge says the repairs were routine, but necessary. He assured stockholders profits would not be affected.

The Bunker Hill concentrator's mechanical and electrical equipment is an example of the most modern machinery in the world. Its compressors supply air around the clock to power machine drills in the Bunker Hill mine.

Galena ore carried down the hill from the mine on a tramway dumps into the concentrator's huge ore bin. There the ore is crushed into smaller and smaller pieces. Once ground fine as sand it goes into a large tank where chemical processes extract silver and lead.

Mick caught up with his brother. He grabbed him by the neck of his jacket and shouted, "Nat, what the heck are you doing?"

"There's gonna be a fight!" Nat's eyes were stretched open so wide that the whites gleamed in the dark like moons. He threw out an arm toward the miners, who had disappeared around a stand of trees. They were headed up the neighboring slash of a valley toward the Last Chance and Bunker Hill mines. "They'll get rid of those scabs, for sure."

"You're crazy." Mick seized the boy by the shoulders and shook him. "This is no place for babies."

"Ouch!" Nat twisted away from him. "I'm no baby. If there's gonna be shootin', I'm gonna see it." He took off up the wagon road. Mick ran after him.

A quarter mile below the Bunker Hill, the group of union men halted in the center of the road. Mick realized it was time for the morning shift to arrive at the mine. But the union men would block their way. Nat had taken to the brush, and Mick followed him. They stopped, out of sight, some fifty yards away.

"I'm not leaving." Nat glared at Mick, his jaw jutting out. "Try to make me and I'll scream."

"All right. But be quiet!" He shoved Nat down behind a stump overgrown with moss and ferns.

A voice sounded from down the hill, and Mick ducked, too. Seconds ticked by; footsteps neared. Mick peeked over the stump and saw half a dozen men carrying dinner buckets coming up the road toward them. The scabs.

"Strikers ahead," said the one in the lead.

"I don't want trouble," said a big man with a drooping mustache.

"Just keep walking," said another.

Mick swung his gaze to the union men. More than a dozen had fanned out across the road. Mick could see Union Secretary Jack Hocking and President Bill Boyles.

The scabs halted ten feet from the line of strikers. The men exchanged words, but Mick was too far away to make them out. One of the scabs raised a fist and shook it. The strikers' rifles stuck out like pins in Mam's pincushion. Even so, two of the scabs stepped up, as if planning to shoulder their way through the union line. Strikers met them eye to eye, and Mick could feel the rumble of rage about to blow.

He shaded his eyes as the sun cleared the mountain peak to the east. Its rays touched the men facing off on the hillside. Boyles jumped onto a stump, putting himself head and shoulders above the crowd.

"We gave you a final chance last night to join the union," he shouted. "If you go back to work at the Bunker Hill, you give us no choice."

A glint of metal drew Mick's glance, and at that moment he saw Da for the first time. He was standing next to Boyles, his slouch hat low down over his eyes. The big revolver he'd pulled from his belt caught the sun as he leveled it at the

Bunker Hill workers. Mick gasped. He grabbed Nat's shoulder.

"I'll tell you what!" Da shouted. "You walk back down that hill inside of four minutes"—he waved the gun as if to point the way—"or you'll be carried down." Drawing his big gold watch from his pocket, he snapped it open.

"I didn't know Da had a revolver." Nat stood up to see better.

"Shh!" Mick pulled him down and held him to the ground behind the stump. He squeezed his eyes shut and waited for the sound of gunfire, but his ears were filled only with the coursing sound of his own blood. The caw of a crow came across the canyon.

After a long moment, he raised his head to look. The scabs had faltered and were backing up a few steps and muttering to one another. Now they turned and started down the hill. A cheer went up from the union men, who took off after them, brandishing their guns.

Mick stared as the men drew abreast of the boys' hiding place. The scabs looked no different from regular union miners. Their faces were drawn up tight, and they walked fast, heading straight down the hill. The union men followed, shouting insults and laughing.

"Da!" Nat stood up and yelled over the commotion.

Mick cringed, but Da turned and walked over to them wearing a huge grin. "What are you boys doin' here?" He stuffed the revolver into his waistband. "You see those scabs turn tail?" he said, clapping Mick on the shoulder.

"Uh-huh."

"Glad to see you taking an interest, son." Da turned to Nat. "But this is no place for a young'un."

"You showed 'em, Da!" Nat jumped out into the road. "You showed 'em good."

Da winked at Mick. "Don't breathe a word of this to your mam. You know she don't take to violence."

Mick nodded, but he thought his father should have been sterner with his brother. Nat was a fool, too stupid to realize that someone could have been killed, too young to remember back to '92, when three union men had died, shot by company guards during a strike.

Mick would never forget it. He'd been only seven, but he'd seen the bodies when they were carried into the union hall in Gem. He'd heard the shooting, smelled the gunpowder, and run through the crowd of little shacks scrunched along Canyon Creek—all there was to Gem in those days besides the Frisco mine and mill.

He'd seen the blood. So much blood, dripping in the mud and spattering on the wood-plank floor of the union hall. So red, and the men's faces so white before they were covered with blankets. His stomach churned at the memory even now as he followed Da and Nat down the gulch.

The scabs picked up speed and headed in several different directions, the union men on their heels.

"Where'd you get that gun?" Nat asked.

"None of your business," said Da. "Forget you ever saw it." His look, with eyebrows lowered in a fierce line, was enough to shut Nat up. Mick nodded, but he knew that neither he nor his brother would forget the big silver revolver.

★★★

Word of the union running off the scabs traveled like a fast breeze through every nook of the canyon. Mick hadn't told a soul, but by the time the bell rang for school that morning every student had heard the news.

Mick wanted to run right to the *Bugle*, start composing sentences to tell what he'd seen, but he couldn't do that without writing about Da's gun. And he didn't want to think about that.

Coming into the one-room schoolhouse, he saw Nat in the back corner surrounded by students. His little brother was crowing like a rooster in the middle of a bunch of hens. His arms waved as if flourishing a gun in each hand. Busy at her desk up front, Miss Sanderson had not yet called the students to order.

"Nat." Mick walked over to him and yanked him by the ear. "Shut up or I'll skin you."

"Let go!" Nat slapped at him, but Mick held on and dragged him away from his audience.

"I mean it," Mick said, clenching his teeth. "Pipe down or you're in big trouble."

"Attention, class," said Miss Sanderson, rapping her desk with a ruler. Dropping his hold on Nat, Mick headed to his seat in the last row.

Few boys stuck with their studies long enough to graduate from eighth grade, as Mick would be doing in June. Most had already gone to work in the mines.

Not me—thanks to Mam, thought Mick as he crammed his knees under the desk. The argument over Mick staying in school was one of the few times Mam's stubbornness had outlasted Da's.

Miss Sanderson wasted no time settling the students down and putting them to work. She started each morning with arithmetic. Mick favored the subjects that came later, literature and history.

"Have you begun research for the end-of-term debate, Mick?" asked Miss Sanderson when she called him to her desk that afternoon.

"Oh, yes, ma'am."

"You're arguing for the free coinage of silver?"

Mick nodded. "'You shall not press down upon the brow of labor this crown of thorns. You shall not crucify mankind upon a cross of gold.'"

"William Jennings Bryan." Miss Sanderson smiled. "Do you have his speeches memorized?"

"No, ma'am. At least, not all of them." Mick shifted from one foot to the other. "It could solve everything, you know. If we got rid of the gold standard and coined silver, the price of silver would rise. The mine owners would have no excuse not to pay union wages."

Crack! Crack! The sharp report of gunshots drowned out Mick's voice. The students jumped up and raced for the windows facing Main Street. Mick ran for the door.

FIVE

Mick rounded the corner onto McKinley Street at a dead run. The image of Da holding the pistol burned in his mind. Had someone been shot?

Wagon teams and men on foot crowded the street. Mr. Tucker had come out from the general mercantile. Standing on the boardwalk, the shopkeeper waved his celluloid visor as he spoke with the dentist and tailor who shared the wood-frame building next door. Every head was turned west, looking down the street to where a lone rider was galloping past the railroad station, heading out of town.

"Hurrah! Good riddance!" Several miners who had been in the saloon chased after the rider. Mick stopped in front of the bank and scanned the crowd for his father.

"What happened?" he asked a man at the hitching rail.

The man was dressed in workworn diggers. He spat tobacco juice and clapped his hands together with a loud smack. "That's one scab won't be back," he said. "He'll be lucky he don't bleed to death. Got a slug in the thigh. Saw it myself."

"Who shot him?"

"I don't know the man meself, but I hear it was one of the Higgins brothers." The miner shook his head and spit again. "Hard ta tell fer sure, with so many firing at once."

"Nefarious thugs," muttered a voice behind Mick. He turned to face a pinstripe-suited man who had come out of the bank. "The whole mob of you ruffians ought to be thrown in jail."

Mick backed away. Godfrey Snipes was a small man, but he stood for the powerful Mine Owners' Association. He was on the payroll of the Bunker Hill and Sullivan Company, owner of the largest mine in the district.

Slipping into the street, Mick headed to the *Bugle*. He'd seen no sign of Da, and the excitement appeared to be over. Most people were going back about their business.

When he reached the newspaper office, Mr. Delaney was coming out the door. "I saw the scab riding out of town," said Mick. "Can I write about it?"

"I want you to go home," said Mr. Delaney.

"Aw—"

"No argument." The editor took Mick by the arm, his face stern. "Promise me you'll go home, or I'll take you there myself."

"But—"

"Mick, a dead newsman can't put out a paper."

"But *you're* not going home."

"If you want to work for me, you'll do as I say."

Mick lowered his head.

"You'll get your chance."

Sure I will. Mick picked out a large dirt clod in the street and kicked it as hard as he could. It bounced ahead of him, and he booted it again, blowing it to bits. Then he walked home, overtaking Nat in front of their house.

"What happened?" asked Mam as soon as they came in. "We heard the gunshots." She knelt before a big tub in the middle of the kitchen, scrubbing laundry on a washboard. Next to her was another tub. Bridey worked beside her mother, putting the sopping clothes through a wooden handwringer. Normally, Bridey went to school, but since Mam had been feeling ill, she was staying home to help with the housework.

"It was a big gunfight!" said Nat. "Pow! Pow!" He pointed his finger and pulled an imaginary trigger.

Mam stood up, dropping the wet dress she held into the tub with a splash.

"It was not," Mick said, glaring at his brother. "It was miners chasing scabs out of town." He hung up his coat and pulled off his muddy shoes. "Nobody got killed."

"Let's pray for an end to this trouble before someone does," said Mam, kneeling again to work in the sudsy water. Her hands rubbed up and down over the washboard, and she began to whisper, "Sé do bheatha, a Mhuire, atá lán de ghrásta, tá an Tiarna leat. . . . Hail Mary, full of grace. The Lord is with thee. . . ."

Bridey joined in, and the familiar words rose also to Mick's lips. But he didn't speak them. He clamped his mouth shut and climbed the ladder to the loft, where he fingered through a stack of old copies of the *Wardner Bugle*, choosing several. He carried them over to the small window that let in the shallow light of late afternoon. There he crouched, reading column after column of Mr. Delaney's editorials on the free coinage of silver, until it grew too dark to see.

He lay down on his bed and thought through the points of his argument. The end-of-term debate would not come for two more months, but he was ready now.

Da did not come home for supper, nor had he returned by the time Mick went to sleep that night. Word had passed from house to house about the meeting at the union hall, and the family did not expect him.

★★★

The next day came on tiptoe. Wardner and the surrounding hills were quiet. All blasting in the mines had ceased. Could it mean that the miners' union held all the aces? Mick wanted to believe it. But the Mine Owners' Association was not above dumping the table, or even pulling a gun to win a hand.

In the schoolroom he could feel the strain. Miss Sanderson had half the boys with their noses to the chalkboard before the morning was over. She dismissed the students early for the noon meal.

Just as the kids tumbled out the door, Anton Scheffer came tearing into the schoolyard yelling. Though fourteen like Mick, Anton had quit school two years earlier. "Somethin's up," he hollered. "Union men took over the train in Burke, and she's loaded with dynamite!"

The children surrounded Anton, shouting questions. Then a few of the boys turned and raced toward the railroad station. Mick wanted to ask Anton how he knew about the stolen train, but he saw Nat taking off at the front of the pack and ran after him. Some of the girls even picked up their skirts and followed.

Mick pounded down Main Street, overtaking the

younger boys. The street was deserted. No pack animals were tied to the hitching rails, no ladies were shopping, no men were trading. The sound of his feet hitting the packed mud was loud in his ears, and his skin prickled as if someone had run a feather down his backbone. A train full of dynamite heading to town? He should be running the other way. It meant nothing but trouble. But he couldn't help the surge of excitement, the sudden hope carrying him along. A show of union strength might force the mine owners to play fair, once and for all.

At the station the tracks stood empty, but Mick saw why the shops of Wardner had closed up. The businessmen were all gathered there, as if waiting for the first mail train at the end of a snowed-in winter.

"You children go home," said the butcher, making a shooing motion at two boys. Mick slipped into the crowd.

"Look! Here it comes," someone shouted. All heads turned east and stared up the tracks. A tiny plume of white came around the far-off curve. There was no sound but the faint chugging of the engine. The smoke unfolded in ever larger billows. The engine, a black dot, seemed to be barely crawling.

Mick looked around for Nat but couldn't keep his eyes off the tracks for long. He blinked as the Northern Pacific train came into view. There were about ten boxcars and a passenger coach. He shook his head and stared. The train looked as if it was covered by a swarm of bees.

"Oh, my gosh!" said a man at Mick's elbow.

"Will you look at that," said another.

Mick felt surprise flow through the crowd as though

someone had stirred it with a spoon. As the train neared the station, he could see not bees but men. Hundreds of men. They filled the cars and hung from the sides. Their long rifles stuck out like quills from a porcupine. Their faces were obscure, shadowed in an odd way.

The train inched closer, belching smoke and raucous cheers. Not until it chugged into the station, steam hissing, could Mick see that the men were wearing masks. He didn't recognize anyone because of the way red bandannas and pieces of buckskin hid their faces. Only their eyes showed through the holes that were cut into the material.

The bystanders surged forward, and the masked men jumped from the train. Smoke stung Mick's eyes. Everything seemed to blur as bodies pushed against him, moving him along up the street. Mick thought the miners must be mostly men he knew, neighbors, friends of Da, but they frightened him in their disguises. Some even wore their coats turned inside out.

Someone stepped on his heels, and he almost went down. All around him boots were clomping on the wood-plank walk. Fighting for balance, he gripped the hitching rail and watched as the first wave of men veered into the nearest saloon, the Royal Galena.

Elbowing his way out of the crowd, Mick headed back to look for Nat. Part of the mob remained at the station. They stood silent now, not moving much. And yet Mick could feel an undertow of tension.

The faceless men had marked themselves with white strips of cloth tied through a buttonhole or around a sleeve. Mick thought that must be a sign of union loyalty. Here and there, there was an uncovered face—the postmaster, the Chinese laundry man, the skinny man from the assayer's office—with jaws tense and eyes darting about like those of a frightened squirrel.

"D'ya hear they put a gun to Hutton's head?" someone croaked in a whisper.

"Yeah. Made 'im stop an' pick up men at every minin' camp in the canyon," another man replied. Mick knew Levi Hutton was the engineer on the Northern Pacific, the railroad that ran through Wardner and on up to Gem and Burke at the end of the line.

"Burbidge has warned all scabs at the concentrator to run for their lives," the man continued. "Even the superintendent—"

A screech of steel sounded loud and long, interrupting this conversation. It sent a shudder through Mick and made him turn his attention to the rear of the train. The door of a boxcar had been thrown open, and men were beginning to unload wooden boxes. Dynamite. Crate after crate came out, hoisted upon waiting shoulders. The miners formed a brisk line, moving the giant powder, as they called it, off the train and stacking it in a huge pyramid on the ground. Mick had seen dynamite plenty of times. This was enough to blow up the whole town, and then some.

SIX

"**N**at!" In the heavy quiet Mick's shout was abrupt and jolting. Where had his brother gotten to? He looked up and down the platform, searching the crowd.

He called again. A few heads turned his way, but no one paid much attention. Everyone seemed to be drifting toward the growing pyramid of dynamite west of the station. The dreadful calm raised the hair on the back of Mick's neck. He wanted to find Nat and get out of there. Dodging elbows, he made his way along the platform, looking for his brother's straw-colored head.

Sheriff James Young stepped up on one of the dynamite crates to speak to the crowd. He had been elected sheriff with support from union miners and other common folk attracted to his working-class politics. Mick knew his straight talk carried weight in the Coeur d'Alenes.

"In the name of the sheriff of Shoshone County and the people of Idaho, I command you to lay down your arms and disperse." His voice rolled out and settled uneasily over the mob. No one moved. No one spoke. Mick thought the sheriff appeared small, even standing up on the box of powder. He felt a tug on his sleeve and looked down into his brother's animated face.

"Isn't this exciting?" said Nat. "Let's get up front."

Mick seized Nat with both hands and half dragged, half carried him back down the tracks.

"Stop," cried Nat.

A miner passed them, a low chuckle flowing from under the bandanna that covered the lower half of his face. "That's the idea," he said. "Better clear out. She's goin' to blow."

"Let go!" Nat squirmed and kicked at Mick's shins, but Mick held fast.

"There's enough giant powder to blow us all to kingdom come." Mick spoke through his teeth, pulling Nat up the street toward the schoolhouse. Whatever happened, they could see it from up the hill, and be a lot safer than they would be down by the tracks.

As they passed the saloons, laughter and loud voices carried into the street. It sounded like Saturday night.

"Mick! Nat!" Bridey ran toward them, her skirts grasped in her hands. "Where's Da? The union hall's empty."

Nat broke free of Mick's hold and shouted, "There's a whole trainload of dynamite!"

"Must be five hundred miners. With guns," Mick interrupted him.

Bridey was panting and her face was flushed. She didn't seem to hear either of them. "Mam's real sick," she said. "I need help."

"Mam? What's wrong?" asked Mick.

"She's burning with fever." Bridey clutched the folds of her apron as though it might run away from her. "She's moaning real loud. She doesn't seem right in her head."

"Mrs. Bielaski?" said Mick. That was the woman who

birthed babies and tended sick people. She lived several houses away from them.

"She's away for a few weeks," said Bridey. Her breath was ragged. "I'm scared. I'm worried Mam'll lose the baby." She looked up and down the street. "Where's Da?"

"We'll never find Da in this mob." Taking Bridey by the arm, Mick turned her around. "We'll just go home and see how Mam's doing. Maybe she'll be feeling better by the time we get there."

Nat looked down toward the train station, then back at Bridey. "Mam's really sick?"

She glared at him.

"Come on." Mick led the way. He took a sharp turn through the livery yard. He'd get his brother and sister home, check on Mam, and then find a safe spot to wait and see if there would be fireworks. Running to keep up, Nat pelted Bridey with reports of the masked miners, boxes of powder, and too many guns to count.

When they reached the house, Mick opened the door and shooed Bridey and Nat in before him. "Mam?"

"*Uhh . . . uhh . . . yeoow!*" The shriek—rising high, then trailing off—came from behind his parents' bedroom door. Mick froze on the threshold.

"*Do something.*" Bridey's eyes were as large as silver dollars.

Mick pushed the bedroom door open a crack and peered inside. Pale sunshine lit the figure under the blankets. Only Mam's head showed. Her black hair hung loose in long curls. Her face was red and puffy, her eyes closed. Mick could see little beads of sweat glistening on her forehead.

Mam thrashed and cried out again. Mick went into the room but stopped an arm's length from the bed.

"She seems hot. Can you take off the blankets?" he asked, his throat constricting so that the words came out sounding like a croak.

"I thought of that, but I was afraid she'd catch a chill," said Bridey.

"Nat." Mick turned to his brother, who had followed him into the room. "Run to the hospital and get Dr. Black." He pinched Nat's chin, tilting his head up. "Go straight there, and come straight back. Understand?"

"Is Mam going to die?" Nat looked as if he was about to cry.

"No, of course not. Now go."

Nat went off running, and Mick tried to think of what to do. Mam couldn't die. How could Nat even think that? "Loosen the covers and take off all but one blanket," he told Bridey.

Mick went outside to the pump and filled a washbasin with water. As he was bringing it into the bedroom, Mam moaned again. Bridey knelt down beside the bed and whispered, trying to soothe her.

"Here," said Mick. He set down the basin and handed Bridey one of Da's clean handkerchiefs. "Bathe her with cold water."

The room seemed to close in on him. He looked away from Bridey's busy hands, from Mam's swollen face. He tried to shut out the moans.

Where was Nat with the doctor? Mick paced the room. He wanted to open the window to freshen the sour air, but he feared a cold draft from outside would be dangerous for Mam.

"This isn't working." Bridey stood and clutched his arm. "What'll we do?"

"*I don't know.*" He shook her off. "You're the one always helping Mam with the herbs and such. Why don't *you* think of something?"

Bridey stared at him. Then her mouth formed a little round *O*, and a light came into her eyes. "Yarrow and comfrey—that's what Mam used when Mrs. O'Leary got the fever," she said. "Mick, go heat the teakettle." Pointing to the door, Bridey waved him out. "When the kettle's hot, we'll steep the herbs. They'll get the fever down and help with the swelling."

Mick went. He stoked the fire in the stove and filled the kettle with fresh water. *Where was Nat with the doctor?*

"Go stay with her while I make the tea," said Bridey, coming out of the bedroom.

Mam lay still now under the light cotton blanket, but her face remained flushed. Mick dipped the handkerchief in the basin and squeezed it out. He turned to wipe her forehead.

Boom!

The explosion thundered through his body like one of Da's punches. He dropped the wet cloth and clapped his hands to his ears. A second explosion followed, rocking the house from roof to floor.

Mam opened her eyes and sat up. "Oh, Mother of God, help us," she cried. "God have mercy on our souls."

SEVEN

Mick ran from the bedroom. He felt a ripping in his throat and heard his own yell, but it was swallowed by Bridey's shrieks. As he flung the front door open, a third explosion hit. He grabbed on to the doorframe.

Outside, smoke blackened the air and debris fell from the sky like hail. A plume of fire shot into the air, dissolving into ash and flying wreckage as it rose. It seemed to come from the Bunker Hill concentrator behind Prospector Hill. The column surged so high he had to tip his head back to see where it topped off. Then the ground and the house shook again.

The dynamite! Before Mick could finish the thought, two more blasts pounded the air, two more tornadoes of smoke and debris churned upward. Then quiet fell, an eerie stillness, and the fog of soot turned broad day to twilight.

"Oh, my God!" It was Bridey. Her fingers fastened on his elbow, her chest heaved.

Mick pried himself loose. "I'm going down there. I'll look for Da and tell him Mam's sick."

He avoided Main Street by cutting through the back lots where the hillside rose steeply to the south. He was coughing by the time he hit flat ground. There was a stream of miners coming his way.

Some men cheered hoarsely, pumping their arms in the air. Others ran as though the devil were chasing them. They headed to the depot and piled onto the waiting train.

Mick climbed a small rise. It was covered with tree stumps, and new spring green was shooting up through the soggy brown of last year's growth. He topped it, then fell back a step. His hands flew to his mouth as he gasped.

The Bunker Hill concentrator lay like a smoking pile of kindling. *The most modern machinery in the world.* The words floated through Mick's mind as he stared. The mill's timbers had been tossed aloft and dropped like a pile of Nat's pick-up sticks. Fire was raging through the company offices and boarding house.

His knees gave way. He sank down on a stump and brushed away the ash that had settled on his cheeks and eyebrows. Though he was more than two hundred yards away, he could feel the heat of the flames, hear the burning wood snap and crackle. The sharp, bitter smell of charred wood and powder stung his nose. A silent line of people stood watching from a distance as the fire blazed, a fire so huge that anyone could see there was no way to stop it. The afternoon sun filtered through the thick air, covering all with a strange, pale yellow light.

The shriek of a whistle followed by the shrill clanging of a bell broke the spell that gripped Mick. He turned to watch the train pull away from the station, heading east. There was a chorus of lusty yells from those on board. *Where was Da? Had he helped light the fuse?*

A cold wind gusted down the gulch and up the back of Mick's shirt. He plunged his hands into his trouser pockets, took one last look at the devastation, and started back toward town.

A crowd of miners filled Main Street. They were hooting and hollering and swigging from bottles. The chorus of an old ditty, "There'll Be a Hot Time in the Old Town Tonight," rang out over the commotion.

At the Royal Galena, Mick slipped through the swinging doors and scanned the room for Da's broad shoulders and reddish blond hair. The place was packed and rang with boisterous voices. He passed by the card tables. Men were three deep at the long polished bar.

"Mick, honey . . ." Mick felt a hand on his shoulder and turned, blushing at the sound of his name in that syrupy trill. "Looking for your pa?" It was Miss Beatrice Beaufontaine. Her lips were as red as a cardinal's wing. She smiled at him. Her fingers, with their scarlet nails, slid easily along his arm. He couldn't speak.

"I ain't seen your pa all day," Miss Beatrice drawled, waving a whiskey bottle in her other hand. "But if he comes in, I'll sure tell him you're looking for him."

"Y-y-yes, ma'am."

"I've got to pour drinks for these thirsty men. You run along now."

Mick ran.

He went down the street to the Iron Horse. Keeping close to the wall, he surveyed the room. Bursts of laughter and the slam of glasses on the bar punctuated the rowdy racket of conversation. Drink flowed, and Old Man Holohan pounded out a jaunty tune on the piano in the corner. Da wasn't there.

Mick ducked out. Where was his father? Had he joined the union mob going back up the canyon on the train? Mick leaned against the post that rose from the hitching rail and tried to think what to do. Better go home and check on Mam. Surely the doctor would be there by now.

★ ★ ★

The house was quiet. Bridey was sprinkling herbs into a pot on the stove. Nat sat at the table, his face all pinched up, as if he was trying not to let the tears out.

"I couldn't find Da," said Mick.

"He's here," Bridey said. "With Mam." She tasted the stew, then put the lid on the pot and motioned with her head toward the bedroom. "He came home right after the explosion."

"I couldn't get the doctor," said Nat. "He wasn't at the hospital, and when the dynamite blew . . ." His voice quavered, and he pressed his lips together and looked down at the gingham tablecloth.

"Mam's doing better," said Bridey. "The herbal tea took her fever right down."

"You should see the concentrator," said Mick. "There's nothing left. They blew it to smithereens."

"Da wouldn't tell us what happened," Nat said. "He went right in to Mam, and he ain't come out."

Bridey sliced bread for supper, and Mick took the tin bowls from the shelf and put them around the table. He placed the spoons next to them, one by one, then the tin cups, then the red checkered napkins. He and Bridey sat down with Nat and waited.

When Da came out, Mick jumped to his feet. He searched Da's face but could tell nothing.

"Let's eat," Da said. "Your mother's sleeping. She won't be up for supper."

"I saw the mill," said Mick.

"Wasn't that grand?" A wide smile lifted Da's bushy mustache and the word *grand* sounded a foot long. "I never saw a prettier sight in all my days." He slapped Mick on the shoulder. "The Bunker Hill boys won't be talkin' so high and mighty now."

Mick tried to smile back at Da, but he felt sick to his stomach. He could hardly believe what he'd seen. The mill, blasted to toothpicks and ash. Maybe there had been men working inside. Had anyone been killed? He sat down to supper, a sense of dread passing through him like a shiver. He wondered again whether his father had helped set off the explosion.

EIGHT

Mick's head ached as he walked to school the next morning, and he rubbed his temples. It was as if a dark cloud hung over the valley and nobody could see it but him.

A current of excitement, like electricity, ran through the talk along Main Street. He heard it in the schoolyard, too.

"Burbidge understands dynamite," said one boy.

"We showed him," said Petey, smacking his palm with the doubled knuckles of his other hand. Mick turned away from the boy who'd lost his da just days ago and tried to shrug off his sense of foreboding.

New blades of grass poked up through the dirt of the schoolyard. Drops of dew shone in the sunshine like rhinestones on a dancehall girl. The day promised spring after a long winter, but it was smudged by the column of smoke rising behind Prospector Hill, where the mill continued to smolder.

"My pa helped place the powder," one schoolboy bragged.

"Mine, too."

"My pa lit the fuse!"

Mick looked from one boy to another, shaking his head. "You think the union'll get away with this?"

"What they gonna do? Arrest a thousand men?" Petey stepped up to Mick, his little face defiant to the last freckle.

"Yeah," shouted the others.

"You can't just go blow up any ol' thing you want," said Mick, but he could barely hear his own words.

"Traitor!" they yelled.

"Knuckleheads!" he yelled back, making a lunge for the boys. They scattered. Stupid kids. Too young to know any better.

But their enthusiasm and sense of certainty pulled at him. He wanted to believe that the union's daring act *would* win this fight. The miners should get a bigger share of the profits for their work. It was backbreaking labor. Dirty. Dangerous. Any day there was a chance you wouldn't come up from the mines alive. Yet it was the mine owners who were getting rich.

His mind was in turmoil. He found it impossible to concentrate on school. When the bell finally rang, Mick ran to the office of the *Wardner Bugle,* where a stranger in a vest and tie stood talking with Mr. Delaney.

"Mick, say hello to Conner Malott of the *Spokesman-Review,*" said Mr. Delaney. Mick knew the *Spokesman* was the newspaper across the state line in Spokane, Washington.

"Hello, young man," said Mr. Malott.

They shook hands. "Pleased to meet you," said Mick.

Mr. Malott turned back to the *Bugle* editor. "You mark my words, those lawless rioters will be brought to justice. There's no room in America for the likes of the criminal scum in that miners' union."

"Conner, you know as well as I do, it's a small bunch of

rotten apples responsible for the violence," replied Mr. Delaney, his voice even.

"The whole barrel has gone to rot." The big city newsman turned on his heel and marched for the door. "Thank God, Steunenberg called in the troops."

Mick gulped as he watched the man put his derby hat on his head and stride out into the street. He swung around to face Mr. Delaney.

"He's a good man—just a bit misguided about labor issues." The editor shook his head but smiled. "Conner and I have been friends for a long time."

"Is it true about the governor?" asked Mick.

Mr. Delaney sighed and pointed down at the type locked tightly in the chase. "Martial Law in the Coeur d'Alenes" read the headline. Mick's eyes raced through the words below it.

BOISE, Idaho, April 30—Today Idaho Governor Frank Steunenberg asked President William McKinley to send in federal troops to restore law and order in the Coeur d'Alenes. "The guilty will be punished," vow state officials, roundly condemning the dynamiting of the Bunker Hill and Sullivan Mining Company mill in Wardner yesterday.

In his mind's eye, Mick again saw Da standing with the union men and holding that pistol. His knees wanted to buckle.

"Do they know who lit the fuses?" Hearing his voice

crack, Mick bent over the chase and pretended to study the type.

"I'm sure somebody knows," said Mr. Delaney. "Today there's a hundred men boasting of the deed. But if and when the case ever goes to court, there'll not be enough evidence to convict the devil himself. The governor and all the federal troops in the West won't be able to drag out the truth of what happened."

Mick felt a bit calmer at the certainty in the editor's voice. He scanned the day's editorial.

Union Right
But Violence Wrong
by Patrick Delaney

The *Wardner Bugle* wholeheartedly condemns the rash violence of yesterday's dynamiting of the Bunker Hill concentrator. Thank God, loss of life was spare. Only one man perished, a union man struck down by a bullet fired by his own kind.

Company men fled the building in time to escape injury and death. However, civilized society must deplore the type of violent, unlawful destruction of property this incident represents.

The demands of the miners' union are right and just. The ends toward which these men unite do advance the common good. However, it is imperative they not lose sight of the rule of law, not relinquish the moral high ground, joining those who would use force of might to further oppression.

As he read, Mick's eyes started to smart. He looked up and saw Mr. Delaney watching him.

"How's it sound?" the editor asked.

"Good." Mick forced the words out over the lump growing in his throat. "It's true, what you say."

But Mick was scared. He was glad to take his turn feeding sheets of newsprint into the flatbed press. The work was repetitious but took concentration and timing. The mind-numbing hum of the press prevented conversation, for which he was grateful. He and Mr. Delaney worked without a break until they had finished the printing.

"I'll do the folding," said Mr. Delaney. "You don't have to stay."

"Should I put the type back in the case before I go?"

"No. Don't worry about it."

When Mick reached the door, Mr. Delaney called, "Mick . . . We've talked before about you continuing your education. Don't let the uproar in town get you sidetracked."

"I won't, sir."

"The Jesuit priests worked nearly ten years to start a college in Spokane. They opened for the first term year before last." Mr. Delaney scratched his head and looked past Mick. "Gonzaga College," he said, and he turned and met Mick's eyes with an intensity Mick felt right down to his toes. "The fathers teach Latin and Greek, science, literature . . . even metaphysics." The editor clapped him on the back. "Think about it, Mick."

"I will."

But all thoughts of college disappeared the moment Mick left the *Bugle*. A train had pulled into the Wardner

Junction station. Blue-jacketed federal troops were marching from the cars and forming up in the street.

Mick stared. Columns of soldiers poured from the train. Each held a rifle upright against his shoulder. *Thunk, thunk.* Boots stomped in perfect time on the platform.

As Mick ran toward the station, he noticed that the soldiers were black. He'd never seen so many Negroes before in his life. Their fierce dusky faces sent a chill through every bone in his body.

NINE

Mick flung open the door of the union hall and searched the crowd for his father. The miners stood in small bunches, all talking at once. He finally found Da near the stove.

"I ain't done a thing wrong," Da was saying. "I'm damned if I'll run for the woods."

"That's what I say," said another miner.

Next to Da, Joe Albinola nodded and hooked his thumbs in his suspenders. "I think Hocking and Boyles are right smart gettin' outta town. The mine owners will be wanting to sic those soldiers on somebody."

Da tugged at his beard. "I still can't believe it," he said. "I thought the whole thing was to throw a scare into Burbidge, like back in '92. When I heard the giant powder go off . . ." He shook his head. "Then the concussion . . ."

Da hadn't known about the blast. He wasn't in on it. Relief surged through Mick, and he hurried to his father's side. "What will the soldiers do?" he asked.

"They can't do a darn thing," said Da. "The mill's destroyed. The men who lit the fuses are gone. Unless they plan to set those darkies to putting the mill back together."

A roar of laughter went up from the men.

"I'll drink to that," said Albinola, and he took a swig

from a bottle of whiskey that he pulled from his jacket pocket. He passed the bottle around, and each man tipped it back. Da drank. He poked Mick with his elbow and grinned, holding the bottle out to him. Mick shook his head and looked down at the floor.

"How we gonna make a man of you?" asked Da. The miners let go with another hearty laugh as Oscar Swenson, a tall red-faced man, took the bottle and finished it off.

Da slapped Mick on the back. "Come on, boy. Let's go home for supper."

When they got home, Bridey had the vittles on and the table set. Mam hadn't left her bed in two days. She was weak, her face and hands swollen, but her fever was gone and her mind was clear.

After the meal, Mick found her sitting up in bed, leaning against the pillows. "Want me to read to you, Mam?" he asked.

She smiled and nodded. As long as he could remember, his mother had ended every day with a Scripture reading, a habit picked up from the Protestant spinster who had raised her when her parents died. Mick remembered stories of how his mam's parents had left Ireland as children, surviving the potato blight and the trip to America on immigrant ships called "floating coffins." But they had died of typhoid in the crowded tenements of New York, leaving his mam an orphan and penniless when she was just a girl. The woman her mother had worked for as a maid gave her a home and even taught her to read.

She liked to say, "It was a miracle I didn't catch the typhoid—but a greater miracle that a Protestant took me in."

Mick went to her dresser and picked up his mother's

Bible. He found Mam's place marked in the Book of Judith. "A tract for difficult times," she murmured.

He cleared his throat and began. "'For thy power, O Lord, is not in a multitude, nor is thy pleasure in the strength of horses, nor from the beginning have the proud been acceptable to thee: but the prayer of the humble and the meek hath always pleased thee.'"

He'd read less than a chapter before her eyelids began to droop and her hands fell limp on the blanket. He closed the book and started to rise, but her voice stopped him. "Pray for your da," she said.

Like prayer is going to take the meanness out of Da? Mick stared at her.

She opened her eyes. "God forgive him. He doesn't mean to hurt you—"

Mick stood up, the Bible falling from his lap to the floor with a thud.

"He—he just loses his temper."

"Why can't he understand that school's important to me?" Mick paced along the side of the bed. "He wants me to be like him. But I'm not."

"Your da had his own dreams once." Mam seemed wide awake now, and she sat up, away from the pillows. "You don't really know him, Mick."

"I know as much as I want to."

Mam went on talking, ignoring his stubborn lack of interest. "When he was younger than you, your da watched his mam and da work themselves to death and still not earn enough to feed their children."

Her hand fluttered in Mick's direction, then fell. "The

mines . . . the union . . . He sees them as security for his family. But when I first met him, he had big dreams."

Mick didn't care to hear about his father's dreams. They had nothing to do with him. But something in the tone of his mother's voice drew his attention. A soft smile curved her lips.

"When I met him, he was going west to be a prospector. He wanted to be his own boss and strike it rich," she said.

"And you left everything to marry and go with him." Mick had heard this part of the story before.

"He was a handsome devil. Always laughing. Always at the center of things. But with me, he was sweet . . . and gentle."

Mick snorted. "What happened?"

She sighed and looked down at her hands on the blanket. Mick thought she wouldn't answer. But she reached for his hand, looked up, and held his gaze.

"Having a family—it's a heavy responsibility."

"That's why he hates me?" Mick stepped away from her.

She shook her head, a shadow crossing her face. "He loves you, Mick."

Mick gave a bitter laugh. "He's got a fine way of showing it."

"Your father seems like a hard man. But I saw how much it pained him to give up his dreams. Maybe he thinks that if you don't have dreams, you won't get hurt."

"So he wants me to spend my life in a hole in the ground? Like him?"

She lowered her eyelids as though she'd closed a door to shut out Mick.

"Well, I won't do it," he said. "I don't know how I'll get the money for college, but I'm not staying here working in some stupid mine." He headed for the door.

"Mick . . ."

He stopped but didn't turn around.

"I'm on your side," Mam whispered. "Don't stop dreaming."

Mick wanted to rush back to the bed and let his mother hold him the way she used to when he was small. But he also had the urge to give the door a swift kick. Run out of the room. Escape this house. Leave Mam and Da and everything connected with them behind. He squared his shoulders and left his mother's sickroom without looking back.

Bridey and Nat had gone to bed. Da sat smoking his pipe, his feet resting on an upended chunk of firewood by the stove. The only sound in the house was an occasional sigh or snap from the fire. Mick sat down at the table. A single electric bulb hung over it. He opened his history book and flipped pages, not seeing them. But soon tales of Marco Polo and the explorer's adventures in the court of Kublai Khan captured his attention and carried him far away.

"I been thinking, lad . . ." Da interrupted, then took a long draw on his pipe, which sparked a fit of coughing.

Mick tensed. He watched his father struggle for air, hack a few times, then throw his pipe down. Da panted, leaning forward in his chair until his lungs began to do their job. Finally, he stood, crushed out the red embers that had spilled from the pipe onto the floor, and sat back down. Mick returned to his lesson.

"Time you stopped wasting yourself at the *Bugle*. This summer maybe you could get on as a shoveler."

Mick stared at him.

"Still a bit skinny, but a month underground with a shovel in your hands'll fix that."

"I don't want to work underground." Mick was startled by his own words.

Da made a fist and thrust out his jaw. "Mining not good enough for you?" A dangerous edge had crept into his voice.

"No. . . . I mean, yes." Mick scrambled to say the right thing, to douse the heat. "Mining is fine. But I like working at the newspaper."

"Hmmph. Delaney can't make enough to pay you. You gotta do *real* work to earn a living."

"I will. But I want to go to school."

"You're finished with school. You've gone eight years." Da got up and retrieved his pipe. He tapped it on the stove and dumped what few cinders remained into the ash bucket. "You got more schooling than your mam and me put together. Time you earned your keep around here."

Mick wanted to argue, but he knew better. At best, he'd get a tongue lashing and extra chores. At worst, he'd end up with a bloody nose and a black eye . . . or two.

"I want to go to college." *Had he said that?*

His father's body grew rigid, and he advanced on Mick. Mick leapt to his feet, almost nose to nose with him. A purple vein pulsed in Da's temple. His large fists opened and closed. "You think I got gold in the bank like those bastard mine owners?"

Mick stepped back from Da's quick, hard puffs of warm tobacco breath.

His father raised a fist. "Get outta my sight," he snarled, shoving Mick so hard it almost knocked him from his feet.

Mick fought for balance, then grabbed his book and climbed the ladder to the loft. He crawled into bed, shaking all over. Even moving close to Nat's warm body did not stop the chattering of his teeth. Suddenly, a thin, clear sound broke into his consciousness . . . Music. A bugle. He willed himself to stillness and listened to the army bugler playing taps down on the flats. The mournful notes faded into the night.

TEN

A pounding on the door woke Mick while it was still dark.

"Who's there?" He heard his father growl from the bedroom below.

"Shea!" Joe Albinola yelled from outside. "Get up. O'Leary's been arrested."

Mick rolled out of bed and pulled on his clothes. The sounds of Da's cursing floated to the loft, followed by his heavy footsteps to the door. His father's friend spoke again, but Mick couldn't make out the words. Nat crawled to the trapdoor and poked his head down the hole.

"Go back to sleep," whispered Mick. "Move—I'm going down."

In the front room stood Albinola, gesturing madly with his hands. "Right outta bed they dragged him. Him . . . Anderson . . . Graham." He wore only red woolens under his coat, which was buttoned wrong, leaving one button with no hole at the bottom. "The darky soldiers took 'em. Said they're arresting all the ringleaders."

"O'Leary ain't no ringleader," said Da, buttoning his shirt and stuffing the tails into his trousers. "Neither is Anderson or Graham."

"A whole column of soldiers is marching up the canyon to Burke and Gem. They're taking away guns from anybody who has 'em."

Mick heard a sound behind him. Nat and Bridey, both fully dressed, stood there.

"Go and spread the word," said Da. "We'll meet at the union hall."

Albinola left, and Da went back into the bedroom and closed the door.

"I'm going with Da," Mick said. "Nat, you and Bridey stay here with Mam."

"I'm going, too," said Nat. "You're not the boss o' me."

Before Mick could answer, his father came out. Mick saw the silver butt of the pistol sticking out of his waistband.

"Bridey, make your mam some tea," said Da. "Keep watch, and if her fever comes back, run and get me at the union hall. Mick, Nat . . ." His tone went stern, and he glared at them. "You go to school or you stay here and help your sister. I don't want either of you about town today."

"Please, Da," said Mick. "Can I go with you?"

"Me, too," Nat said.

Da pulled on his coat, his back to the boys.

"I won't get into any trouble," said Mick. Whatever was going on, he wanted to see it firsthand. This was real news. Maybe Mr. Delaney would let him write a story for the paper. He'd never say that to his father, though. "Sounds like the union should make a show of men."

Nat caught his father's hand. "Please, Da. I want to come."

Da ran his fingers through his younger son's hair and

smiled. "Nat, you got more spunk than sense. Stay here and do as Bridey says." He glanced at Mick. "If you're coming, let's get a move on."

Mick felt goose bumps rise on his arms and back as he closed the door behind him. Immediately, he wished he'd worn his winter coat. Though it was the first week of May, a light snow had fallen. It was hard to know when winter was whipped in the Coeur d'Alenes. Seemed it could rise up and overtake spring at any time. But Mick figured once the sun rose the snow would begin to melt.

At the union headquarters a fire was roaring in the stove. A dozen men were gathered around it, and Mick and Da joined them. More miners arrived. Some had rifles, or the bulge of a pistol under their coats, but most were unarmed.

An angry voice rose above the hubbub of half a dozen conversations. "We've got to make a stand!" A thick man with a huge misshapen nose rapped on the bottom of a washbasin with his pistol barrel. "How many men are armed?" he barked.

"That's Joe Devine from the Burke union," Da whispered to Mick as a shout went up and several men raised their rifles above their heads. Mick knew the Burke union was the most radical in the district. Each town had its own local union, but recently they had all united and joined the Western Federation of Miners.

"The mine owners have their army. We need a workingman's army," said Devine, waving his pistol.

"Let's not get carried away." It was Albinola on the opposite side of the room. "We're law-abiding citizens. We have nothing to fear from the army."

"Rubbish," said Devine. "Ain't they hauled off a bunch of union men already with no evidence of wrongdoing whatsoever? Ain't they marching right now for the mining camps of Burke and Gem, armed to the teeth?"

"We gotta stay calm," answered Albinola. "We don't want bloodshed."

"We can't fight the army," Oscar Swenson joined in. "That'd be pure suicide."

"He's right," said Da, and most of the men agreed. Two of them, as burly as Devine, offered the Burke man a chair and told him to cool down.

Cookie Dolan came through the door with a pail of sourdough and started pouring flapjacks on the stovetop. Soon side pork sizzled there, too. Mick noticed that the smell of breakfast lightened everybody's mood. As soon as the food was ready, they ate, and more than a few relaxed and seemed to enjoy the circumstances. A poker game sprang up. Several miners sat down, propped their feet on chunks of firewood, and snoozed.

Near noon a boy ran in the door yelling. It was hard to tell if he was frightened or excited. "The soldiers are coming!" he shouted. "They're marching up the street."

Mick ran to the window at the front of the union hall, but he couldn't see out. Miners who'd gotten there first blocked his view.

"Sure enough," said one. "Here they come."

Quiet fell on the room, and Mick could hear the sound of marching feet. Not the crisp *thump, thump* one might imagine, but more of a squishy *blurp*, squashy *plup* in the spring mud.

"Halt!" The marching stopped.

"By order of the United States Army"—the command came in a clear, loud eastern accent— "All men in the union hall come out with your hands up."

As if planned in advance, the men around Mick moved—not toward the door to the street but to the rear of the hall. Da gripped Mick and grunted in his ear, "Stay here." Then he was gone with the whole bunch out the back door. Only one, a white-haired man with a peg leg, remained in the room along with Mick.

"Come out or we're coming in," they were ordered again. And then the soldiers must have noticed the exodus from the back of the building. "After them! They're getting away up the hill!"

A rush of footsteps pounded past the building. At the same moment, the front door flew open with a smash, and two blue-coated soldiers leapt into the room.

Mick stared up the long barrel of a rifle into the dark brown eyes of a soldier. He barked at Mick. His teeth flashed white. But Mick couldn't make out his words. He stood frozen, afraid he might piss his pants.

"Hands up!" This time Mick understood the words and raised his arms, trying to stop them from trembling. The soldier held the gun on Mick with one hand and patted his shirt and trousers with the other. Mick stared at the man's weapon. He feared his knees would buckle and the soldier would shoot him dead.

Then the soldier seized him by the upper arm and pulled him along. Mick stumbled out the door. They followed the other soldier as he dragged the old one-legged man out into the street. They stopped in front of the prancing hoofs of a glossy black stallion.

"Fall in with the prisoners," ordered the white officer who was astride the spirited horse. He stood in the stirrups, pulling on the reins, and holding a pistol high. His blue coat showed not a speck of dirt. Gold braid adorned his shoulders, and brass buttons and medals decorated his broad chest. A neat iron-gray mustache topped his lips. His eyes blazed at Mick.

Mick tried to speak, to say he was innocent, but no words came out. With a rough push, he was directed to a line of captive miners. He lurched into place behind the peg-legged man. Each prisoner was flanked by two soldiers. Mick's two guards stood so close he could feel the warmth of their bodies through his jacket. They stared straight ahead, though, as if he weren't there, and Mick tried to calm the trembling in his limbs.

Bursts of gunfire came from the side of the narrow canyon behind the union hall, where some miners had scrambled for safety amid the stumps and rocks. An uneven line of soldiers returned shots from positions lower down. The air smelled of sweat, gunpowder—and fear.

Though it was a chilly day, Mick began to perspire as he watched a knot of miners break cover and run up the hillside. With a shout, the bluecoats advanced, rifles blazing. Two or three union guns answered, but they were clearly outnumbered.

"Surrender!" The officer's shout echoed in the sudden quiet. "Surrender, or we'll show you no mercy."

A figure with his hands up rose from the protection of a

stump. Mick blinked. It was Joe Albinola. Another followed, and then another. The soldiers ran forward seizing the union men as they gave up. A pile of rifles, pistols, and knives formed in the middle of the street as they confiscated the miners' weapons, unloaded them, and threw them in the heap with a clatter. *Where was Da?*

Mick bit his tongue and scanned the hillside. He craned his neck to watch as the soldiers escorted miners back down to the street one by one.

"You can't arrest us," shouted one man as he was dragged into line.

"We ain't done nothing," yelled another, and a general cry went up.

The officer on horseback fired his pistol, splitting the air and quieting the clamor.

"Silence!" he roared. "You are under arrest by order of the United States government."

"He's only a boy."

Mick turned at the sound of his father's voice. Da broke free of two soldiers and lunged toward him. Hands snatched hold of Mick's upper arms.

"Let him go!" Da shouted. "He's got nothing to do with this."

A soldier struck Da in the stomach with his rifle butt, and Mick cried out. Da doubled over with a grunt and fell to the muddy street in a heap.

"Da!" Mick twisted, tried to jerk away, but the soldiers at his sides held him fast.

"Forward . . . march." The command rang out, and the remaining union men were prodded into line. The column stepped forward, the soldiers in lively precision. Mick looked back. Da lay still. A soldier stood over him. Then Mick couldn't see him anymore.

The column stopped abruptly at the butcher shop, and two soldiers went to the door and rapped on it. There was no answer. Mick cringed as they kicked the door down and went inside. They came out hauling the butcher, still in his bloody apron and letting loose a string of cuss words.

At the Iron Horse Saloon, next to the butcher shop, the soldiers arrested half a dozen miners; one was dragged out still holding a hand of cards. They took the bartender and even Old Man Holohan into custody. It was the same at the laundry and at the livery barn. The soldiers halted any grumbling by the prisoners with a glare and a raised rifle stock.

When the troops arrived at the *Wardner Bugle*, Mick started to shake again. It began in his hands and traveled up his arms and into his body until the whole of him shook so hard he couldn't stop it. A soldier kicked in the door of the newspaper office and two of them went in. *Not Mr. Delaney! He's not even in the union.* Mick felt something like crazy laughter rising in his throat. He wasn't in the union, either, but they had captured him. They seemed to be arresting every man in town. He struggled for control, but a choking sob escaped from him. A gun barrel poked his ribs, and he looked up into the eyes of the soldier on his right.

"One shot," said the man, his face fierce, "and you's dead in the mud."

If they hadn't been holding him, he might have fallen to

the ground. It took everything he had to straighten his back and hold his head up. He tasted blood and swallowed hard. He must have bitten his lip.

The soldiers who'd entered the newspaper office came out. "Place is empty, sir," said one, saluting the man in the saddle, who motioned them to continue down the street.

They passed by the bank without stopping, and the offices of the lawyer who represented the Mine Owners' Association. But at the small building owned by Kerr, the union attorney, they halted. Kerr had come out to meet them, and Mick felt his hopes rise.

"Who are you?" Kerr said to the officer. "And by what right do you hold these men?"

"I am Brigadier General Henry Clay Merriam, and you are under arrest."

"Where is the warrant? The Constitution of the United States guarantees every citizen safety from unlawful seizure."

"The Constitution is void in the Coeur d'Alenes," said Merriam. "This district is under martial law, and I am sheriff, judge, and jury." He nodded at the soldiers next to him, and two stepped forward to grasp Kerr by the arms.

"Unhand me." Kerr's voice remained calm but hard as steel. "You've no warrant for my arrest."

Without a word, Merriam wheeled his horse away. A sergeant pulled his pistol and aimed it right between Kerr's eyes.

"Forward," he ordered.

The union lawyer didn't move so much as a muscle. But the troops at his side lifted him off his feet and jostled him into line. The column started moving again. *Left, right, left, right.*

This couldn't be happening. What would they do with him? With all of them?

The column of prisoners stopped when it reached the flat ground behind the dry-goods store. It was where the Wardner baseball team played.

Another company of soldiers was stationed around an old barn at the edge of the field. Mick's guards let loose their hold on him, and he risked turning his head slowly, looking through the crowd, hoping for a glimpse of Da. A whack like the one that had felled Da wouldn't kill a man, but his father could be injured badly. Had they left him lying in the street?

Mick shivered. This was like some story in a book. How could it be happening to him?

ELEVEN

"**F**all in!" yelled the officer on the fine horse. The soldiers walked back and forth, lining up the miners as if they were a company of recruits. Mick found himself near the back of the formation. He guessed that a hundred men had been arrested and were now arranged on the field.

All around him men were muttering to one another, but a trooper stationed close by ordered them to keep silent. The air had warmed in the noonday sun, and a fly buzzed around Mick's head. He was afraid to swat it away under the watchful eye of the guard, and he began to feel a bit dizzy. What had happened to Da? he wondered as he shifted his weight from one foot to the other.

On the far side of the field, soldiers marched in with another large group of prisoners. A whisper swept through the ranks. This group of men had been arrested upriver in Burke. Some of the new men jeered at the troops, and shouts rose throughout the crowd.

"Let us go!"

"We're innocent!"

Two pistol shots rang out, and the soldiers moved in closer to the prisoners, repeating their orders for quiet. Reluctantly, the men obeyed.

★ ★ ★

As the day wore on, Mick began to fear that he'd keel over. His legs kept going to sleep, and his stomach growled with hunger. The only relief came when he took his turn at the privy. One man at a time was allowed to walk to the outhouse behind the dry-goods store. Returning to his place in the ranks, Mick tried to hold on to hope. This was all a big mistake. Soon the soldiers would let them go.

But by suppertime the army had herded in yet another bunch of captives, these from the mining town of Gem. No food was offered, and more than one prisoner fainted, falling to the ground where he stood. Then a soldier would rouse him with a dipperful of cold water and get him back on his feet. A heavy gloom settled over the ranks.

Mick's expectations rose when the soldiers separated some of the men and marched them across the field. Then he saw that they were being directed into the barn that stood on the south side of the clearing. To keep alert, he began to count the men as best he could. More than two hundred disappeared into the building.

By dusk Mick found himself walking on numb legs toward a shed near the barn. He was lined up with about fifty other prisoners. One by one they stepped into the small wood-frame building.

The smell of chicken manure burned his nose as he hunched over and entered through the low door. Prodded by a rifle butt, he stepped on the heels of the man in front of him, who swore loudly. It was dark in the chicken coop, but Mick could sense it was crowded.

He'd had nothing to eat since the flapjacks at the union

hall early that morning. But now, as the stink of sweat and anger mixed with chicken manure, he was thankful his stomach was empty. His eyes adjusted to the dark, and he looked for a space against the wall. His shoes squished in the soft layer of manure covering the floor.

A chill wind blew down the canyon and whistled through cracks in the walls. All Mick wanted to do was sit down, but the filth on the ground sickened him. The first prisoners in had claimed what little straw there was, making dry nests for themselves.

Mick made his way to the wall and leaned against the rough boards. He bent forward so as not to bump his head on the rafters. Every bone in his back cried out in protest. When the complaints and curses of the men inside let up for a moment, he could hear the steps of sentries passing outside. Wrapping his arms around himself for warmth, he tried to sleep.

There was no telling how many hours of the night had passed when rusty hinges screeched and a light shone at the end of the shed. The shape of a man appeared in the doorway. The man stumbled in. Two more men followed. "Hey, don't step on me, you lubber!" someone bellowed.

The figure in the lead only groaned and continued feeling his way through the bodies of the sleeping miners. Though the man was bent over, something in his posture was familiar. It was Da.

Mick rose from his crouch against the wall intending to call out to his father.

"Ouch!" he cried instead as his head bashed against a beam of the low roof. He sank to his haunches and cradled his head. Bright splashes of pain swirled in front of his eyes.

"Mick . . ." croaked a voice. "Lad."

Mick opened his eyes and saw Da stretching out a hand to him. The pain in his head suddenly exploded into anger. He'd been worried that the soldiers had killed his father; but now that he saw him alive, he was mad. *This is all your fault*, he wanted to scream. Da moved in close and put his arms around him, but Mick shrugged away.

"You all right?" Da asked.

"I'm fine," Mick said through clenched teeth. "I'm freezing my arse off in a pile of chicken shit. Not to mention half the army is standing guard outside waiting to shoot me."

He thought he heard Da start to chuckle, but if so, it turned into a groan. His father settled down next to him, wheezing with convulsive jerks.

"You gotta . . . get out of here," Da hacked. "I'm sorry, lad. Those bastards." He interrupted himself with a cough. "I never should have let you go to the union hall. Didn't know it would come to this." He let loose a string of colorful words, then groaned again and fell silent.

As the pain in his head receded, Mick remembered the soldiers knocking his father to the ground. "You hurt bad, Da?"

"Naw—no more'n a couple cracked ribs."

Mick leaned back against the wall, listening to the snoring around him. Every muscle in his body hurt, his belly gnawed itself in hunger, and the cold bit through his clothing.

He thought he'd never sleep that night, but he must have, for the next thing he knew it was morning, and Da was shaking him. A bright square of light marked the open door of the shed, and men were filing out. Mick stood and stretched his arms and legs as much as he could in the cramped space, waiting his turn. Men outside were shouting, and something metal clanged. Coming into the daylight, Mick blinked and rubbed his eyes. Then he saw what was causing the uproar. Soldiers had lined up pig troughs in rows. They were emptying porridge from huge army kettles into the troughs. Other soldiers on horseback stationed about the field were ordering the prisoners to eat.

Miners shouted, thumping the air with their clenched hands, and several charged the soldiers, only to be lashed with horsewhips or whacked with rifle stocks. Mick stared at the nearest trough.

"We're not animals," he yelled. "You can't treat us like this." He rushed at a soldier, wanting to pound him with his bare hands, but Da and another man pulled him back. "Easy," cautioned Da.

The soldier came close and spoke directly to Mick. "I know's it's bad eaten' from a trough. We jus' don' have nuttin' else. Maybe by supper . . ."

Supper! Mick felt panic rising in his chest. They meant to keep them here at least the rest of the day. He looked at the grim faces of the silent miners around him, then down at the lumpy oatmeal in the trough.

One by one, men squatted at the pig feeders, dipping their cupped hands in the porridge. Rising steam carried the smell of cooked oats. Mick's mouth watered. He elbowed his way in between two bearded miners and started scooping with both hands.

TWELVE

It was two days later that Mick realized the soldiers had no intention of letting him or any of the union men go free. That morning the armed guards had put them to work building their own stockade.

Mick dropped his hammer and inspected the stinging sores on the palm of his hand. Three nights locked in the chicken coop and now a day of hard labor had left him exhausted, but with plenty of time to think.

He simmered at being locked up. To pass the hours when he couldn't sleep in the filth of the shed, he turned his mind to his plans for college. Working next to Da, he nursed his anger but kept a lid on it. The men here respected his father and gave Da food and dry straw at night because of it.

He picked at the blisters that had been formed and broken open by the hammer handle. They oozed blood. "Da, we have to get out of here," he said.

Da drove a nail home with one more swing of his hammer and turned to Mick. "Let me see that," he said taking his son's hand. "Lad, you should've told me."

Mick tried to pull his hand away, but Da gripped it. From his pocket he took his handkerchief, filthy as it was, and wrapped it around Mick's palm and tied it. "Hold the boards while I nail," he commanded.

They hoisted a board and placed it next to the one they had just finished securing. Mick held it in place with his uninjured hand. Da pounded in the nails with an easy rhythm. The calluses and muscles from years of working underground with a pick or drill made this carpentry work like a holiday for him and many of the other miners.

But they were in no holiday mood. They'd been slaving since sunup. Mick guessed there must be nearly a thousand men arrested now. Both the ground floor and the haymow of the horse barn had been filled with prisoners. As the soldiers dragged in more men from surrounding mining camps, they commandeered boxcars from the railroad and turned them into makeshift jails.

"Water!" A soldier carrying a bucket and dipper made his way along the sturdy fence they were building. He let each man drink his fill before moving on. Mick sighed and tried to let all his muscles go limp as he stood waiting his turn. His right hand throbbed. When the soldier reached him, he drank long and deep, wanting the cool water and the moment of rest to last forever. Then he handed the dipper to Da, not looking at the soldier's face, not trusting his ability to control the fire coiled and waiting in his belly.

Even as he worked, Mick watched. The soldiers had grown more lax as the number of prisoners increased. Several men had escaped. If a chance came, Mick would run for it. He could leap the fence, still less than waist high, and maybe get away. The length of the pen he and Da were building faced the back side of businesses on Second Street.

A wide-open space stretched from the stockade to the cluster of buildings. But if he had thirty seconds, Mick thought, he could make it to freedom.

As the sun reached its height in the sky, several women and children appeared outside the barricade. Families had gathered the day before, inquiring about their menfolk. Some brought blankets and vittles to pass through the soldiers' lines to their husbands and sons. The guards kept a sharp eye on the interchanges, inspecting blankets and bags and limiting visiting time.

Now one captive miner spotted his young wife. "Caroline!" he yelled. He dropped his hammer and thrust his arms over the rough planks of the fence. The woman ran forward and grasped his hands. A soldier hurried toward them. He allowed the couple to embrace for a brief moment, then grabbed the man by the shoulder.

"Back to work."

The miner picked up his hammer, and the young woman stepped away. Covering her face, she dissolved into tears.

Mick searched the gathering crowd for Nat or Bridey. He saw Da looking, too. But neither said a word as they continued lifting the boards and nailing them into place. Another team went before them, digging holes and setting the posts. A dozen crews worked at different points on the stockade. Other prisoners carried lumber, and a large number were building long, low buildings at the four corners of the enclosure.

The day wore on like an endless dusty road. Mick's thoughts drifted, and his bones ached with weariness. When the soldiers called a halt to the construction and started to pour food into the troughs, Mick wondered if he even had the strength to eat. He wanted to lie down right where he stood, but instead he followed Da. He took the piece of bread handed him and sank to the dirt next to the trough. The man beside him ate like a starving animal, using his fingers to pick up the stew when his piece of bread was gone.

"Eat, lad," said Da. "You'll need your strength."

Mick felt clumsy using his left hand, but his right burned with pain. The stew had little flavor. He could barely recognize the carrots and potatoes. But as he ate, he began to feel better. The talk around him started to make sense. Most of the men talked of escape. Mick noticed Joe Devine, the Burke man with the ugly nose. He urged the men to take up their hammers against the soldiers. "Some of us will die, no doubt," he said. "But they can't shoot us all. Some of us will get through. We can rally those hiding in the hills, then come back and make a real fight of it."

"I just want to go home and see my wife and kids," said one man. Others nodded. Disbelief showed on Devine's face. He shook his head as if they were silly children and walked away.

When they had finished eating, a number of prisoners were put to work sloshing out the troughs. Mick and Da drifted with a group of men toward the half-finished fence. Soldiers stood guard along it every fifty feet.

Women and children had come right up to within an arm's length of the divide. Mick saw a plug of chewing tobacco change hands, a blanket, a loaf of bread, and a chunk of roast beef.

One man grabbed a copy of the *Wardner Bugle* from the

outstretched hand of a boy. Mick sidled over to him, drawn by the newspaper banner, so sweetly familiar. When the man sat down to read, Mick peered over his shoulder at the headlines.

HILLS FULL OF FUGITIVES

EVERY MAN FOUND IN BURKE, GEM ARRESTED

HUNDREDS DETAINED IN BULLPEN NO DUE PROCESS

HERDED IN BY NEGRO TROOPS

Mick bent closer to read the fine print.

Mr. Delaney would publish the truth for all to see. The *Wardner Bugle* would help bring this nightmare to an end.

WARDNER, Idaho, May 3—Early today soldiers began the wholesale arrest of men believed to be connected with the Bunker Hill outrages. At first the colored soldiers took into custody only the men named in the warrant filed by prosecutors in the arson and murder case. But later when it seemed most rioters were heading for the hills, they began arresting any union men they could find. The net soon widened to include suspected union sympathizers.

Eighty-five-year-old Jack Holohan was among those incarcerated, as well as a fourteen-year-old boy known by this editor to be completely innocent. Saloon men, teachers, preachers, and even the postmaster have been arrested.

Mick swallowed hard and blinked. Mr. Delaney meant him. The editor would vouch for him. Surely the soldiers would let him go.

"What's it say?" asked the man holding the paper. "Do you read?" He thrust the *Bugle* into Mick's hands, and Mick read the next column aloud. It was Mr. Delaney's editorial condemning the government for sending in federal troops to settle local affairs.

Negro soldiers of the Twenty-fourth Infantry Regiment proved themselves heroes at San Juan Hill. They established themselves as loyal and courageous Americans by fighting for their country and surviving yellow fever in the jungles of Cuba.

How dare the government pit them against their own countrymen in the Coeur d'Alenes?

It seems the powers that be desire to fan the flames of racial unrest while at the same time illegally incarcerating innocent workingmen—men simply desiring a just share of the profits produced through their own sweat.

Mick glanced at the nearest soldier with new eyes. Had these Negroes really helped capture San Juan Hill? Mr. Delaney had told him of labor strikes in the eastern coalfields where soldiers and miners had fraternized, the soldiers later refusing to move against the union men. This, he was sure, would never happen in the Coeur d'Alenes. The line had been drawn the minute the soldiers marched into town, and it would not be crossed.

"Da!"

Mick recognized Nat's cry and leapt to the barricade. He grasped Nat's hand, never imagining he could be so glad to see his little brother.

"Nat . . . Nat . . ." Da's voice was hoarse as he, too, clung to the boy.

"Back!" shouted a soldier. He stepped in and pushed Nat out of reach. Mick kept his eyes on his brother as the crowd jostled him. Nat was speaking, but so many people shouted back and forth that he couldn't hear him.

"To the barracks." The order came from a captain striding along the inside of the stockade. "Turn in for the night." The soldiers herded the men away from the townspeople. Nat was yelling now, and his words carried over the confusion. "The baby's coming! Mam's bad. Real bad."

THIRTEEN

Mick threw a look at his father. Had he heard Nat? Yes. Da's face was still and hard as rock.

"We'll escape, Da," Mick said softly. "We'll get out tonight."

Da squeezed Mick's shoulder. "Lad . . ." he said, then shook his head.

A lump grew in Mick's throat. He'd get them free. He'd do it somehow.

They shuffled into the chicken coop with the other men. They had tried to make the place habitable by scraping the worst of the manure to one side. Mick scrambled to the far edge of the shed, where he had made a nest of straw against the wall. Wrinkling his nose at the stench, he ignored the grumbling around him and tried to think how he and his father might escape. His thoughts went around in circles, always coming back to the insane idea of tunneling out of the chicken coop. Even if they could find something to dig with, it would take days to channel underground far enough to get away.

He heard a soldier patrolling outside in the falling darkness, pacing back and forth. Could he tackle an armed guard without getting shot? If he somehow knocked the soldier out without alerting other troops, they might have a chance. But it seemed too risky. Any noise and more guards would come running. Mick shifted, trying to ease his sore back where it pressed against the rough boards of the wall.

"Ugh," he grunted. Something had jabbed him through his trousers, spearing him in the hip. He twisted, heard a splintering sound, and felt another twinge of pain. The board behind him moved.

Mick froze. *Could a board in the wall be loose?* He gingerly felt his rear end and with a jerk freed the sliver that had pierced his trousers. He rubbed the tender spot, deciding it wasn't the worst thing he'd suffered so far. Then he settled his weight against the plank. *It moved.* Just a little, but enough to give him hope.

He waited until heavy snoring signaled that the men around him, including Da, had fallen asleep. He'd never heard such a racket. Then he listened for the footsteps of the sentry. When they had passed, he put gentle pressure on the board. Nothing happened. He pushed again, harder.

Screech. Mick froze at the sound of the board squeaking free of the nail. But it must not have been as loud as he feared. Nobody stirred. The soldier went by again, and Mick knew he would have to time his movements carefully.

With his fingers, he dug away some of the mire beneath his feet, making room for the board to swing outward without catching on the bottom. About a foot and a half from the ground, the vertical one-by-twelves were nailed to a horizontal two-by-six timber. That's where the board had come loose.

Mick now stood, his head bowed under the low roof, and

felt the board where it connected to a second two-by-six near the top. It was nailed firm. He tried to squeeze his fingertips into the crack between the boards but couldn't. Kneeling down, he again turned his attention to the lower end of the plank. He worked with a slow, steady rhythm. First he listened for the tromp of the sentry's feet, then he pushed carefully on the board and wriggled it from side to side, all the while counting in his head to time the soldier's return.

The nails seemed to hold fast forever. And Mick's fingers grew numb in the cold. Was he being too cautious? Should he just get his hands around the board and wrench it free?

"Halt!" The shouted command rocked Mick back onto his heels. But a loud guffaw followed, and he realized the soldiers were changing watch. It must be midnight. He heard murmured conversation for a few minutes and then the sound of one man leaving. Mick rested and warmed his hands in his armpits. He'd have to wait and see the new guard's routine.

It was hard to keep his eyes open. He bit his lower lip, wiggled his toes, flexed his fingers. One, two, three, four, he counted, waiting to hear the pacing soldier pass again. But the soldier did not return. Or had Mick fallen asleep? Confused, he got to his feet and strained his ears. He counted to sixty and still no footsteps. He stooped and pried the board with all his might. The nails gave a low groan, and it came free.

"Da!" He shook his father's shoulder.

"Arrgh . . . what?"

"Shh." Mick put a hand on Da's cheek to quiet him and

spoke close to his ear. "Da, listen. I've loosened a board in the wall. It's a way out."

Da sat up. But as he showed his father the hole he'd created, Mick's hope sank. He could slip out through the opening, but his father would never fit. They'd have to free another plank. Why hadn't he realized that? Mick dropped and clawed at the dirt below the next board. *Stupid. Stupid.* Da leaned over and covered Mick's hands with his own, stopping his frantic digging.

"Go ahead," he whispered.

"But Mam needs you."

"Go." His father's tone was low but urgent. Mick nodded. Da let go, and Mick rose to a crouch, moved the loose board aside, and slid through the narrow opening like a weasel getting away with a prize pullet.

He gulped in the fresh air. Clouds covered the valley; the night was black as coal. He hadn't taken one step when a hand clasped his shoulder.

FOURTEEN

Mick lay on his side. His hands and feet were tied behind him. He blinked his eyes but saw nothing except blackness. Wet seeped into his clothing from the packed earth floor beneath him. He was too cold to shiver. His cheek, planted on the damp ground, was numb.

He tried not to think about where he was. Underground. Just the thought brought terror rising in his throat, threatening to choke him. The soldiers had marched him away from the chicken coop and taken him down near the railroad tracks. They had threaded through rows of tents where the regiment lay sleeping. His anger turned to panic when they arrived at the ruins of a cabin with an old root cellar. The cabin had burned down several years earlier. Mick and the other boys from town had explored the ruins, but he'd never ventured into the cellar—too scared it might cave in. His captors tied him up, carried him down the wooden steps into the dark, and left him—slamming the door and pulling out the latchstring.

When he landed in the root cellar, he had fought to free himself, and eventually just to hold his head off the dirt. But weariness had overwhelmed him. Now he felt like a limp bundle left to rot in the dampness with a few forgotten potatoes. He could smell them. As foul as putrefied potatoes could be, they were better than chicken manure.

But that was the only thing better. This was his worst nightmare come true. He squirmed, trying to get some blood flowing in his arms and legs. He had to focus, had to think of a way out. He'd been careless, escaping from the chicken coop and walking right into the arms of the sentry. He had wanted to kick and scream as one soldier tied him up and another arrived with a hammer. But he had remained still as they nailed the plank back into place; the shed was more secure now than the day it was built.

The silence of the cellar echoed in Mick's ears. No sounds penetrated the thick moss-covered door. If he shouted for help, no one would hear him. He decided not to waste his strength yelling.

The leather cords binding his hands and ankles would be the place to begin. He had started working to free his hands as soon as the soldiers left him, but this only made the thongs cut into his skin.

Now he tried again, twisting his hands, straining his tingling fingers to reach for the knots. He wriggled his wrists into a crossed position, left over right. He figured he could work at the binding with the fingers of his right hand, but he found they were so numb he couldn't feel the knot.

Maybe he would die here. He had no food or water. He felt cold enough to freeze to death. Who would rescue him? So many men had been arrested that their names hadn't even been taken. One prisoner would never be missed. Surely Da would ask about him. But Da was a prisoner himself. Nat? Nat was plucky, but he was a child. Mr. Delaney might be able to do something, but how would he even know that Mick was missing?

He thought of his dream to go on to school, maybe become a newspaperman like Mr. Delaney, maybe a writer like Shakespeare or a politician like William Jennings Bryan. His worst fear had been that he might end up like Da, working all his years deep in a mine. Now he'd be lucky if he didn't die underground in this smelly hole. His mind drifted to his mother. Would he ever see her again? *He had to find a way out.*

Mick pulled again at the ties binding his wrists. Could he reach the knots at his ankles? If he could stand up and walk around, he'd get warmer and he might find a tool. He arched backward, stretching his bound hands toward his feet.

It hurt badly, but he was able to touch his shoes. He felt like an acrobat he'd seen once in a traveling show. His fingers were dead, so he paused and flexed them back and forth, trying to get some feeling into them. With all his strength he reached again, and this time he felt his trouser leg. *Stretch a bit more. Yes. The leather knot.*

Mick had no idea how long he struggled with the knot, huffing in the dank air. He worked, then rested, then worked some more. He noticed the effort warmed him a little. He wouldn't allow his mind to wander but thought only of the job at hand. When he finally felt the cord slip a bit and the knot loosen, he was so tired that he barely registered his success. The tie fell away, and he lay there, too weak to move.

He felt warm now. He was sitting by the stove at home,

and his mother was serving him steaming potato soup. It tasted so good. He must be dreaming. But he didn't care. If it was a dream, he didn't want to wake up. Then he remembered. His legs were free. Or was that a dream?

Mick rolled over on the cold ground. His legs *were* free. He sat up and tried again to stand. He managed it after several attempts by scooting to the wall, crossing his ankles, and slowly pushing upward. He wobbled a few steps back and forth like a baby learning to walk. The cellar was small. He could stand upright but could take only five or six steps in each direction. The wooden bins lining the walls were crumbling, although the steps from the door seemed solid.

As Mick moved about the cellar, his mind cleared and he felt stronger. Though he couldn't see much in the dark, he began to search for something sharp for cutting the ropes on his hands. If there were cracks to the outside, it must still be night because no light showed. And yet it seemed he'd been locked in the cellar for days.

He fumbled around the floor and in the corners, feeling only squishy potatoes and rotting boards. Even a nail might help, but he couldn't find one. Figuring he had covered the entire cellar, he gave up and slumped down on the steps to the door. Sighing, he let his head sag to his chest. Would he ever get out?

A trembling started inside him and grew like a fast-moving storm from the west. Panic whirled through the dark, taking his breath away. He gasped, clawed at the invisible force choking him. A sound like the roar of a cornered animal filled the air. He was on his feet, turning, charging up the steps. Pain hit him like a blow from a hammer. Bright orange and red flashed before his eyes. He whimpered. His whole body throbbed. He had smashed into the cellar door with his shoulder.

Slowly, one simple fact sifted to the top of his consciousness. *The door had moved.*

A crack showed along the side of the door—not bright, but the glow of dawn, an opening to the outside. Mick winced as he put his bruised shoulder against the thick wood near the latchstring hole. He ignored the pain and leaned on the door with all his strength. The wood of the latch groaned. Again he felt the slight give. He backed up, turned his other shoulder to the door, and charged again. This time the wood splintered, the latch gave way, and he felt the door give. He rested, panting, and then pushed the door up until it fell open.

Squinting in the morning light, Mick raised his head and looked out. Straight ahead he could see dozens of white army tents between the river and the hills, the nearest only a hundred yards away. Smoke drifted up from campfires, and he could see blue-jacketed figures moving around. A group of hobbled horses munched what grass they could find in the foreground to the north. He turned to look south. The remains of the burned cabin lay twenty feet out. Beyond that, open space with some scrub and stumps separated his cellar from the side of the canyon, which rose softly another hundred yards away. The trees had been logged; lumber had been much in demand as the town grew.

He pulled back into the cellar to think. What if he crawled? From a distance he'd be hard to spot if he kept low.

Squirming his way across the flats on his belly and up the side of the canyon would take a long time. And with his hands tied behind his back, it'd be rough.

Mick looked out the door again. Maybe he could find something in the debris of the cabin to cut the leather cords. The horses had moved, spreading out toward him. Could he escape in that direction? Screened by the horses, he could run to the railroad tracks. He'd be in plain sight as he went up and over the tracks, but then he'd be hidden the short distance to the river. He could follow the river up through the canyon to the other end of town, then double back safely toward home.

With a glance toward the army camp, he crawled from the cellar opening, heaved the door closed behind him, and loped toward the tracks. He didn't move fast for fear he might spook the horses. When he reached the farthest one, he stopped, speaking to it in a low tone. He stooped, peered under its neck toward the tents—and almost cried out. Two soldiers had left the camp and were walking briskly toward the cellar. Mick could see that one carried a dipper. They must be bringing him water, maybe even breakfast. He wouldn't wait to find out. He leapt up the railroad embankment and hurled himself across the tracks and down the other side. Without pausing, he ran toward the thicket of juniper and wolf willow on the riverbank.

Mick crouched, listening for anyone coming after him. All he heard was the drumming of a ruffed grouse, distant sounds from the army camp, and the nicker of a horse. He took off again, dodging between young cottonwood and aspen trees. The long flattened leaf stems of the aspens trembled at the breeze of his passing. It was harder than he expected as he headed upstream, scrambling over the rocks and through the brush without his arms for balance. *But he was free!*

FIFTEEN

Mick had longed for a drink of water since those early moments in the cellar, but now, as he scurried along the river, thirst came on him like a sickness. Should he chance a drink? Nobody had taken a drink downriver from the mills for as long as he could remember. The water was so full of tailings from mining that it never ran clear; rather, it was a murky gray, foaming in the eddies and rock pools. And so he ran on. He was bound to reach a side stream feeding into the river soon. He could drink then.

A log bridge crossed the river just past the railroad station, where the old Montgomery Creek Road came into town. Mick stopped and hid in a thicket of water birch. He looked out between the drooping catkins. Would soldiers be guarding this route? He didn't see anyone, but watched for a few moments longer. Sure enough, two soldiers appeared. They sauntered toward the bridge, pivoted, and went back the way they had come. When they were out of sight, Mick made a dash for the bridge, keeping low. He slid into the darkness under the logs, in water up to his knees, crouching.

Listening for the guards' return, he waded under the bridge to the far side. He heard their voices and then their footsteps. The sounds faded. His muscles tensed as he got set to make a run for cover upstream. Then he saw something that stopped him. A tin can bobbed on the water toward him. Its lid was still attached, and bent at an angle. He saw the gleam of a sharp edge—just what he needed. Could he get it before it floated by?

Staying in the shadows under the bridge, he stepped deeper into the water—and yelped. The South Fork of the Coeur d'Alene river wasn't deep, even now with the spring runoff beginning, but the water, which was up to Mick's crotch, was cold as ice. He locked eyes on the tin, willed himself toward it. One more step. Yes! The can bumped against him.

Unable to grab it, Mick bent his knees and with a shiver lowered himself into the river up to his elbows. Stretching, pushing his aching muscles, he worked his hands up his back and to the side, making a space between his left elbow and his body. Exerting every ounce of his concentration, Mick maneuvered in the current. The tin can bobbed, then floated into his trap. He pinned it under his arm, and sighed with satisfaction.

His legs were so numbed by the icy water that he struggled getting back to shore. Once there, he huddled, shaking with cold, and tried to think. When he heard the sentries retreating, he dropped the can and sank to the ground on the rocky embankment.

With little feeling left in his fingers, he managed to locate the sharp edge of the lid and struggled to find a way to use it to cut his leather bindings. Every time the marching feet and voices of the bluecoats returned, he froze, clenching his teeth to stop their chattering.

As the footsteps faded, he went back to work. He shut his eyes and tried to ignore the soreness in his shoulders and arms, the exhaustion, the painful tingles in his fingers. There had to be a way to hold the makeshift knife in order to rub the leather against the cutting edge. He tried to lodge the can between rocks, to hold it with one hand. But nothing worked.

If only he had eyes in the back of his head, then he could see what he was doing. He was muttering a few curse words under his breath when an idea struck him. He waited for a moment, then planted himself on the can like a hen sitting on an egg. Feeling for the razor rim sticking out behind him, he stretched the leather that bound his wrists across it and began to saw.

Back and forth, back and forth. He feared he might be sawing his flesh rather than the rawhide rope. He wouldn't know it—his hands were that dead. But he kept on. Then, suddenly, he toppled backward. His wrists were free. He lay a moment, panting, and stretched his arms slowly out in front of him.

Oooh! It hurt. Like a thousand needles jabbing his hands and arms. But he'd done it. He was free.

Mick heard the soldiers' footsteps again. When they were gone, he peered from under the bridge. All clear. He gathered himself and sprinted to the grove of young cottonwoods fifty yards upstream. There he paused, sucking in deep gulps of air and stretching his arms above his head, then swinging them back and forth to loosen his shoulder muscles.

A stick snapped in the underbrush. The noise startled him. He was a fugitive. He'd better get moving.

Animals had made a faint path through the foliage

along the bank, and he followed it. He tried to balance the need for quiet with the need for speed. He wanted to put as much distance as possible between him and any soldiers who might be on his trail.

Though he couldn't see the town, the river ran close enough to it that he could hear the rumble of wagons and the stomp of horses—and he could smell the stench of rotting rubbish, of human and animal waste warmed by the sun. It wasn't yet noon, he thought, casting a look at the sky. He was starving. He wanted nothing more than to go home, sit down to a hot meal of Mam's beef-and-potato pasties, and fall into bed. But it would be folly for him to walk into town in broad daylight. He couldn't take any chances. He walked on.

The sounds of civilization faded as Mick came to a small stream rushing into the river. The mills dumped their tailings into the river, but most of the creeks that emptied into the South Fork of the Coeur d'Alene remained clear. Stepping up his pace, he followed the stream into the woods a short distance and stooped down for a drink.

Cupping his hands, he scooped up the water and took in huge gulps. *Ah!* Water had never tasted so good. He drank his fill.

In the distance were the snow-covered peaks that fed the stream, but down where he was the sun felt warm on his back and he relaxed a moment. Soon his clothes would dry, and he would stay warm enough if he kept moving. Turning away from the stream, he circled east through the foothills and gullies. He planned to swing wide around the town and come in from the south. It would mean a steep climb up the east side of Wardner Peak, over the top, and down again. But it seemed the safest route.

Mick kept up a good pace, tromping through the ferns. He filled his lungs with the sweetness of cedar and the damp, heavy scent of decaying wood and leaves. Chipmunks scattered in front of him, babies fresh from their burrows. He allowed himself to forget that he was running from the law, that Da was in prison, his mother ill, and the whole town turned inside out. The hours flew by as he climbed the peak. He broke out in a sweat in the afternoon sun, but it was easier going in the higher elevations, with less underbrush to impede him.

When he reached the crest, he could see far below where Milo Gulch emptied into the flats. The scene didn't seem real, with its miniature buildings and tiny white army tents. He moved faster now, heading down, trotting when he hit open space. He could no longer ignore the possibilities that awaited him at home. A prickle of fear ran through him as he thought of his mother. Was it only yesterday that Nat had told them she was in labor? Less than twenty-four hours—but it seemed an eternity. He picked up his step.

Mick knew he was almost home when he sighted a familiar old prospector's cabin along a little stream he had passed many times while out hunting for game. His stomach growled, and he could almost smell roast venison. There might not be much for supper tonight, but it would be good enough just to be home. No longer worried about the crackle of sticks under his feet or the swish of branches as he passed, he broke into a run.

SIXTEEN

The sun had set, and the house stood in shadow. Mick slowed to a walk the last hundred yards. He had never been so happy to be home. He followed the footworn path leading to the slightly sagging stoop. As he climbed the two steps, a sudden fear came over him, and he paused. Then pushing aside his apprehension, he swung the door open.

The main room of the house was dark and empty, though a fire blazed in the stove. Dirty dishes lay piled on the drainboard, and a chair by the table was askew. Buckets of water sat on the floor, and a pot full to the brim bubbled and hissed on the stovetop.

"Mam? Bridey?" Mick called.

He heard steps in the bedroom, and Bridey opened the door. With the glow of light behind her, Mick couldn't see the expression on his sister's face. But as he glimpsed the set of her head and shoulders, his empty belly squeezed into a hard knot.

"Oh, Mick! I'm so glad you're home," Bridey said, her voice near cracking. As she flung herself into his arms, he glimpsed blood on her sleeves and skirt. Clinging to him, she collapsed into sobs. "Mam's real bad."

"Has the doctor come?" he asked, patting her back.

Bridey straightened and drew back. Even in the faint light he could see her eyes flashing.

"There is no doctor. Mam's dying, and it's those soldiers' fault. They arrested Da . . . and you. They arrested the doctor. They've put the whole town in that pen."

A tiny wail from the bedroom punctuated the end of her sentence, and Mick seized his sister by the shoulders.

"The baby?" he asked.

"Yes. It came this morning."

"You said Mam's dying." Mick shook her. "Speak to me."

"The baby's fine. It's a girl," Bridey answered. "She's tiny, but she's beautiful."

Mick pushed past her and went into the bedroom. His mother lay on her side in bed. The baby nestled at her breast. Mick stopped short. The air was thick and sweet, heavy with the odor of fresh blood. The bedsheets lay on the floor, soaked red brown. A pile of towels and rugs were covered with the same dark stain. Mick fought for control as the room swayed around him. He felt Bridey's hand on his arm.

"What?" he gasped.

"The bleeding won't stop. Mick, I've done everything I know. She just keeps bleeding and bleeding. . . ." Bridey sank to her knees and dropped her face into her hands.

Mick turned from her to his mother on the bed. So pale, and not even a flicker of an eyelash. He stepped closer. Was that a pulse in her neck? Yes, barely. Frustrated at the nipple, the baby screwed up its tiny red face and let out a string of cries that sounded like the desperate mewing of a kitten.

Mick felt as though a swift river current was dragging him under. He fought his sense of drowning and pulled Bridey to her feet.

"Water—tea—she needs fluids," he said.

Bridey shook off his hands and glared at him. "I've tried," she said. "She won't drink—"

Bam, bam, bam! They both jumped.

"It's the front door. You go," whispered Mick. "Maybe the soldiers have come after me." He pushed Bridey out and closed the bedroom door. He pressed his ear against it.

"Good evening, Miss Shea. Is your father home?"

The voice was unmistakable. It was Snipes. What could *he* want?

"Moira, then. . . . Surely I can speak to *her.*" Mick seethed at the sound of the Bunker Hill man using his mother's given name. He heard the door close and his sister's low voice, then Snipes's again, much louder and closer. "Indisposed, you say? A likely story. You Sheas are no better than beggars. You've not paid rent in two months, and I'll no longer take promises. I want money, and I want it now."

Mick burst through the door and faced the short balding man, who was dressed all in black. "Get out," he said. "You have no right to come into our house, and no right to threaten my sister."

Snipes stepped back a pace, raised his eyebrows, and lifted the black walking cane that he held in his right hand. "*Your* house, you say? This house is owned by the Bunker Hill and Sullivan Company, and as of now I put you on notice to vacate the premises."

"No!" gasped Bridey. "Mam's sick. We can't— She mustn't be moved."

"We'll pay the rent," said Mick. "You'll get your money."

"I'm here for it now," said the company man. "Hope you don't mind if I sit while I wait." He pulled out a chair from the table and sat down, placing his cane and hat across his knees.

Mick stared at him, then glanced at Bridey. She moved toward the hutch. Mick knew she was after the china teapot on the top shelf. It held all the money the Sheas had.

"How much do we owe?" asked Mick.

"Forty dollars a month. You owe for the last two months. That's eighty dollars—plus forty for this month." Snipes had picked up his cane and was stabbing the floor with it, emphasizing each phrase.

"One hundred and twenty dollars?" Mick felt his knees go weak. From the corner of his eye he saw that Bridey had paused, holding the teapot in midair. They both knew it rarely held more than ten dollars. In the strained silence that fell, the baby's crying came clearly from the next room. Mick motioned Bridey to go to the baby. She put the china pot back in its place and left the room.

"Mr. Snipes," said Mick, stretching himself up as tall and straight as he could. "We'll pay in full. Da will bring the money to the office."

Snipes laughed. His high-pitched cackle carried no humor, and his small black eyes reminded Mick of the way a weasel looks when stalking a hen. "Now, boy," he said, "we both know your da and the rest of those union rioters are locked up. They're not going anywhere. If you can't pay up, you've got to move out."

Bridey came out of the bedroom carrying not the baby but a heap of blood-soaked towels. She walked to the back door and dropped them into a washtub. As she went by, Snipes started and his face paled. The baby's cries grew shriller and seemed to fill the room. "Eh . . . the blood . . . is your mother's?" he asked.

"We told you Mam isn't well," said Mick.

The man got to his feet and fidgeted with his hat and cane. His eyes flitted about the room. "I didn't know your mother was . . . uh . . . um, so ill," he said. "I see you can't move out."

"Just give us some time," said Mick. "We'll pay the rent."

"The hutch." Snipes pointed to the finest piece of furniture in the room. "I'll send some men to take a look at the hutch and see what it's worth. Perhaps it'll cover some of what you owe." He walked to the door and went out.

"He can't take Mam's hutch! And he can't make us move out," said Bridey.

"No," said Mick, "he can't." But he knew as he said the words that they were not true.

SEVENTEEN

The baby was quiet now. Bridey had gone into the bedroom and closed the door. Mick tried not to think about what she might be doing in there. He cleared the shelves of the hutch, taking down the china teapot, a small silver-framed looking glass, a brown jug holding dried wildflowers, and the tin plates and cups the family used for meals.

Mam loved the hutch. Sometimes she stood and stroked its wood as though it were something alive. "If eyes are made for seeing," she often quoted Ralph Waldo Emerson, "then beauty is its own excuse for being." She'd be broken-hearted to find it gone. Well, there was no other choice. Not unless Da came home and things got back to normal somehow.

Mick went to the stove and poked at the fire. He added another log and watched the flames until they flared up and began to lick along its bark. Closing the stove, Mick sat down at the table. His whole body felt heavy with exhaustion, and he rested his head on his arms. He'd go in and spell Bridey . . . later. Was it only an hour ago he'd come home?

The baby's cries woke Mick before he knew he'd been sleeping. Bridey came out of the bedroom carrying the little one.

"She's starving," Bridey said. Her face was cinched together in worry lines, as if with a drawstring. "Help me."

Mick stood up but backed away as she neared. "I don't know anything about babies." He looked at the squirming, screaming bundle and wanted to turn and run.

"Just hold her." Bridey sounded beyond weary. "Hold her tight and rock back and forth. I'll make her a sugar teat."

"A what?"

Bridey ignored his question and thrust the baby at him. Feeling clumsy and awkward, he took hold, his arms out in front. So light! She weighed less than a five-pound bag of meal.

"Don't drop her!" Bridey looked as if she would grab the baby back. "Hold her against your chest, like this." She showed him. "Your heartbeat will comfort her."

Mick did as Bridey said, but the baby still cried. He jiggled her and watched his sister. She laid a square of clean muslin on the table and placed a spoonful of sugar at its center. She gathered the corners of the cloth and twisted them together, trapping the sugar in a bulb at the end. Then she dipped the bulb into the steaming water on the stove and let the excess drip off. Mick marveled at her. How did she know all this?

"Give her here," said Bridey, sitting down. Mick handed her the baby, sighing with relief. Holding the newborn in the crook of her arm, Bridey waited for the sugar teat to cool. Then she nudged the corner of the baby's mouth with the bulb of sugar, and the little one turned her head, latched on, and began to suck. Mick slumped into a chair opposite Bridey.

"How'd you get out of the bullpen?" she asked him. "And why'd you get arrested in the first place? Is Da all right?"

He answered her questions, making it a short story and assuring her their father was all right. "Where's Nat?" he asked.

She seemed to crumple. "I yelled at him. He left and hasn't come back."

"That brat. I'll pound him—"

"No. . . . He was upset about Mam, about Da being locked up, about everything. Mam was in labor, and I . . ." She broke down then, finishing her sentence in a sob. "I just did the best I could." She didn't have a free hand to wipe away her tears, and they ran down her cheeks and dripped onto the baby's blanket. Mick looked away, casting his eyes about the room for a handkerchief or anything. He went to the shelf over the drainboard and came back with a checkered napkin.

"There, there." With a fumbling hand he dabbed at her face and her red-rimmed eyes.

"Mick, will you sit with Mam?"

He tensed.

"Mick . . . We can't leave her alone."

He closed his lips on the biting words ready to spill out. It wasn't Bridey's place to tell him what to do, even if she *was* right. He knew nothing about babies or sick people. The sight of Mam and all that blood had frightened him more than anything he'd been through. This new Bridey giving him orders just made it worse. But as much to get away from her as anything, he rose and went to sit with Mam.

She opened her eyes when he came through the door, and he hurried to the bed.

"Mam."

Her lips moved, as though she was trying to smile. They were chapped and cracked.

"Do you want some tea?" Mick asked.

Her mouth made a no.

"Water?"

She gave a slight shake of her head.

"You need to drink, Mam."

"No . . . good," she said.

Mick had to lean close to hear her. "You have to." He took her hand and squeezed it. It was cold. Too cold. He looked around the room. He had to do *something*. He saw a teacup that was half full. Carefully he measured out a spoonful of the liquid and placed it on his mother's parted lips.

Some dribbled from the corner of her mouth, but he thought she must have swallowed some, too. He gave her another, and then another. She gurgled, then choked. Her weak cough sent the tea flying back out. He wiped her face with the corner of the sheet and got ready to try again.

"No . . . use," said Mam.

It hurt so much to see her like this. His mouth filled with a taste so bitter he wanted to spit it out. Though she was a small woman, Mam had always been strong, hauling water for washing, chopping wood, and turning sod for the garden.

"I'll do whatever you want, Mam."

"Mick . . . sit with me."

"Yes, Mam." He pulled the chair close and sat down. She looked at him, her eyes huge and bright, clear blue with flecks of gold from the lamplight.

"Da?"

"Da's fine, Mam. Just fine." He grasped her hand.

"I . . . won't . . . see . . . you . . . college," she said.

"You will, Mam. Don't say that." Mick squeezed his eyes shut. He wasn't one to pray much, but now without thinking he whispered, "God, make Mam well. *God, you have to.*"

"Mick," she said, and he opened his eyes.

"The baby . . . Nat . . . Bridey. Take . . . care of them."

"I can't." Mick gulped. "Mam—don't go!"

But she closed her eyes and didn't seem to hear him.

Mick knelt by the bed and put his cheek close to her mouth. He waited, nerves stretched taut, for the puff of her breath. Yes, ever so slight, like the brush of a blade of grass against his skin. She touched him with what life she had left.

The anger came like the stroke of an ax, and just as sharp. It filled Mick, threatening to gag him. Da should be here. Damn the soldiers! Damn the union! Damn Da! Mam needed him. They all needed him. Mick's whole body went rigid, like one in a fit. He was squeezing Mam's hand with a viselike grip, but she didn't feel it.

"No. . . ." Letting loose his anguish and anger, he pounded the mattress with all his might. "No, no, no."

"Is she dead?" Bridey had flown into the room and was shaking him hard by the shoulder. "Stop that, Mick."

His anger died as quickly as it had come, leaving him

hollow, leaving him as empty as the wind wailing through an abandoned mineshaft. He sank to his heels and dropped his forehead to the mattress.

"Mam . . . please. Don't leave us," sobbed Bridey, kneeling beside him and laying her head on their mother's breast.

Together they watched each breath she took, each bit of life ebbing. Until there was no more.

★★★

Bridey washed Mam's body and dressed her in her Sunday gown. Mick learned to make the sugar teats and to rock the baby, just so, to quiet her cries. By the end of the long dark night, he had come to like the feel of the tiny warm bundle in his arms. He fastened his attention on this scrap of life, this searching mouth, as if there was nothing else. He didn't let his mind travel beyond the immediate task of feeding, and occasionally changing, the motherless baby.

Bridey finished her work and closed the bedroom door behind her. She held the infant's basket, which she placed on a chair drawn near the stove. Mick wrapped the sleeping newborn snugly in her blanket and laid her inside the basket. The little bundle rose and fell. The rhythm of her breathing seemed to Mick so tenuous and yet at the same time indomitable.

"Let's name her Moira," he said.

Bridey nodded. "We have to tell Da what's happened," she said wringing her hands. "And Nat."

"Yes."

They sat across from each other at the table as the first golden light of morning shone into the room. They ate bread and drank tea in silence. Then Bridey washed the pile of dirty dishes, and Mick chopped wood and filled the wood-bin.

"You'll have to go and tell Da," said Mick. "I can't risk the soldiers seeing me. I'll stay here with—with the baby. When you're back, I'll go make arrangements with Father Becker."

Bridey turned away and wiped her face with her apron.

"Mam's in a better place now. Don't you worry, we'll be all right." Even though he said this, Mick didn't believe it. He didn't know what to believe. One minute he felt numb clear through and the next his chest filled with an ache so painful it watered his eyes. "We'll be all right," he repeated. "Tell Da we'll get him out of there."

When Bridey had gone, Mick sat by the stove and watched Moira sleeping. Her helplessness frightened him. She wouldn't stay alive on sugar teats for long. She needed milk. They'd all need food. And the rent . . . Snipes would be back. Even if Da got free, he'd have no work. Mick couldn't sit and wait for Da. The baby depended on him—Bridey and Nat did, too. He'd have to take care of them all. But he had no strength left, and he fell asleep in the warmth from the stove.

"Mick! Mick!" Nat was shouting and shaking him. Nat's cheeks, smudged with dirt, went in and out of focus. "How did you get away?"

Mick's grogginess faded in the face of Nat's excitement, and Mam's death came rushing back to him. He stood and grasped hold of his young brother. "Where have you been?"

His sharp tone froze Nat, but only for an instant. The

boy jerked away toward the door. "I don't answer to you," he cried. "You're not my mam."

"Mam's dead."

The words fell like rocks dropped into a well, a deep well. Mick felt them falling, falling.

"You're lying!" screamed Nat. He got to the bedroom door before Mick could block his way. He ran and threw himself on Mam, still yelling.

Mick thought the solid coldness of the body would bring Nat to his senses, but he clung to it, refusing to let go, refusing to quiet down. Mick caught him around the middle with one arm, prying loose the boy's grip and carrying him from the bedroom.

Moira was screaming now, too. Nat slapped at Mick's head and kicked at his legs.

Mick dropped him to the floor in a lump. "Settle down."

"I hate you! I want Mam!"

Mick ignored him and picked up Moira from the basket, rocking her, trying to stop her wails. Nat seemed to notice the baby for the first time. He shut his mouth with a gulp and stared.

With one hand, Mick wrapped sugar in the muslin and dipped it in water. "Shh, shh," he whispered. "Just a minute, little one." He blew lightly in her wrinkled face, and she stopped crying to catch her breath. He tickled her lips with the teat, and she started sucking. Mick relaxed, a strange feeling seeping over him. It felt good to be able to satisfy the baby.

Nat had come near. He was watching Mick's every move. Mick held out a hand to him. Nat ignored the hand.

"I'm hungry," he said.

"There's bread in the tin."

"Don't want bread. I want flapjacks and fried eggs."

"Look, Nat, all we've got is bread."

Nat gave him a sullen stare, but he took out the loaf of bread, cut off a piece, and began to eat it. Bridey came in then and Nat ran to her, breaking into tears. He cried while she held him and crooned, petting his head.

"How's Da?" asked Mick.

Bridey pressed her lips together and shook her head. Moira had gone to sleep, and Mick got up and put her in her basket.

"He's relieved you got away," said Bridey. "He heard the soldier take you when you escaped from the chicken coop."

"Did you tell him we'd get him out?"

"Yes. But I don't think he heard a thing after I told him about Mam." Bridey sat on the floor, holding Nat. She rocked back and forth. "What'll we do, Mick?" she whispered.

He didn't know. He felt like a bug caught in the eddy of a stream, going round and round, flailing its limbs, unable to swim free.

EIGHTEEN

Raindrops turned into small rivers and ran down Mick's neck as he prodded the borrowed jackass along the road. It was steep and rutted. Once again, he checked the ropes that held the pine box in the cart. Bridey, Nat, Father Becker, and Mr. Delaney walked behind, their heads down. Several parish women wrapped in black shawls completed the mud-spattered procession. Mrs. Bielaski returned to town and had offered to stay at home with Moira.

None of it seemed real to Mick, not even the soaking rain. Putting one foot in front of the other took all his attention. He'd been working all night building the box for Mam. Father Becker told him the army had agreed to send soldiers to make the coffin and dig the grave.

"Why can't they just let Da go?" In his bitterness, Mick had shouted at the priest, "Those soldiers ain't touching anything to do with Mam."

He had labored through the afternoon digging at the graveyard, and then he had walked down to the sawmill for lumber. Mr. Olafson had refused his promise of payment for the pine boards, insisting they were scrap. He'd also lent Mick the jackass and cart.

Mick tugged again at the animal's lead. It had stopped

and closed its eyes. He got it moving again. At last, the road leveled off. Mick could see the pile of fresh earth ahead, way to the east end of the open field. It was a new cemetery, the land chosen by the citizens a few years earlier when the town hemmed in the small graveyard on the flats. Mick had picked a plot at the edge, near the spreading branches of a huge cedar.

He led the way, and Mr. Delaney helped him take off the lashings and lift the box down. It was heavy for the two of them, but they settled it on the ground near the open grave without a bump.

Bridey came and stood on one side of him. Nat stood on the other.

Father Becker pulled a silver vessel on a chain from his robes, opened it, and struck a match. The incense smoldered, and he closed the lid and began to chant. "In Nomine Patris, et Filii, et Spiritus Sancti . . ."

Mick made the sign of the cross and fixed his eyes on the fresh-cut wood of Mam's casket.

Father Becker swung the chain up, down, and sideways, spilling the pungent smudge from the incense all around the coffin. "Requiem aeternam dona eis, Domine, et lux perpetua luceat eis," he prayed. *Eternal rest grant unto her, O Lord, and let your perpetual light shine upon her.*

"Amen," they all answered.

The graveside service was short. Father Becker had offered the requiem mass at the church earlier. Now he helped Mick and Mr. Delaney lower Mam into the ground.

Mick thought he should feel more, but he felt only the smoothness of the wood on his hands and the dampness of the rain on his head and shoulders. He was the first, after a nod from Father Becker, to pick up a handful of earth and drop it onto Mam's coffin. It made a soft, hollow thump that echoed in his heart. He watched Bridey, then Nat, do the same, their faces white and expressionless. The others followed, and Father Becker said the closing prayer and sprinkled holy water into the grave. "In paradisum deducant te angeli; in tuo adventu suscipiant te martyres. . . . aeternam habeas requiem." *May the angels lead you into paradise; may the martyrs receive you at your coming. . . . and may you have eternal rest.*

"Amen."

"Hail Mary, full of grace . . ." whispered the neighbor women as they took Bridey and Nat in hand and led them toward home. Father Becker offered to return the donkey and cart, and Mick found himself relieved to be left in the quiet with a job to do. Mr. Delaney helped with the shoveling.

They didn't hurry, and when the *thwunk* of each shovelful hitting wood gave way to the softer *whup* of earth returning to earth, Mick began to think of what lay ahead.

"I need work," he told Mr. Delaney as they walked back to town.

"I'm sorry," the editor said. "I wish I could hire you. I just don't have the money. Especially now."

"I wasn't asking you." Mick stopped and faced him. "I just thought maybe you knew of something."

"I thought you planned to go on to school."

"I do—I mean, I did." Mick started walking again. "The rent is due."

Mr. Delaney laid an arm across his shoulders, but they

reached the *Bugle* office before he said anything. "The only paying work in the Coeur d'Alenes is underground. The miners' union is banned. The mine owners have joined together and instituted a permit system. It's backed by the new sheriff the army has installed, and nobody works without the proper papers."

Mick's head started to throb as the meaning of Mr. Delaney's words sank in. He'd never wanted to work in the mines, but even if he did, now it would mean betraying the union. Only scabs would be signing on.

"I'm sorry," said Mr. Delaney. "I wish I could help you."

Mick nodded and dumbly accepted the editor's handshake.

"I'll let you know if I hear of anything," Mr. Delaney called after him as he left.

The hearty smell of beef and vegetables met Mick at the door when he arrived home. Mrs. Bielaski sat with Bridey at the table drinking tea. But she stood as Mick shook the rain from his hair and took off his sodden coat. "I go now," she said.

"Thank you so much for the stew," said Bridey, handing the woman her black shawl.

"Is not so much. I like help more. We have same trouble with menfolks locked up." She pinched Nat's cheek. "You be good boy and help sister."

"Much obliged for your kindness, ma'am," said Mick as he opened the door for her.

"Worse before better. An' good Lord knows is true," said Mrs. Bielaski, pulling her shawl around her and stepping off the stoop into the mud.

Mick closed the door and looked about the room at what remained of his family: Nat, sullen and still by the stove, Bridey, jiggling the whimpering baby with one arm and putting tin bowls around the table with the other. His stomach grew queasy, and he swallowed hard. The stew smelled good, but he feared he wouldn't be able to keep it down.

"Mrs. Bielaski's cow has come fresh," said Bridey, setting out spoons next to the bowls. "Moira needs the milk. She won't live on sugar water. I can mix the cow's milk with corn syrup so she won't throw it up or get the runs."

Mick stared at his sister. She spoke so sure of herself, and it annoyed him.

"I'll talk to Mrs. Bielaski," he said, taking a seat at the table. "Come, Nat. Let's eat."

Nat sat down, but Bridey did not. She stood across the table from Mick. "I've already bargained with Mrs. Bielaski for milk," she said. "I've given her the money in the teapot. I know it's all we have, but . . ." Bridey bent her head over the baby in her arms and kissed its forehead. She swayed back and forth and made soft cooing sounds.

Mick balled his hands in his lap and let his feelings rumble up like a thundercloud. It felt better than being scared, better than the awful grief. Suddenly, he pounded the table. The tin bowls rattled. A storm of emotion—excitement and release, as well as fury—swept through him. "We needed that money for the rent!" he shouted.

Bridey tossed her head. She met his eyes. He was the one to look away.

"Let's eat," he said.

The stew tasted delicious. Chunks of tender beef, potatoes, carrots, and thick gravy. Mick had eaten the like of it all his life, but the flavors had never seemed so satisfying. He lost himself in the warmth, the feeling of fullness growing in his stomach. He emptied one bowl and then another, pulling into himself, taking refuge in the simple comfort of good food.

Then without a word, he put on his coat and went out.

NINETEEN

The stink of mud mixed with manure and slop tossed out the back doors of the saloons assaulted Mick's nose as he neared the center of town. Dancehall music sounded in the street, short bursts of gaiety, as men went in and out of the swinging doors of the Royal Galena. A crowd of men dressed in diggers, stood outside the bank.

Mick gaped at them. Hadn't all the miners gotten locked up in the bullpen? He didn't recognize any of them, and by the sound of their voices he decided they weren't Coeur d'Alene men. He crossed the street to the livery stable to ask about work.

"Sorry," said Mrs. Graves, wife of the liveryman. "Lots of men coming in on the train, but they don't need horses or wagons. They ain't goin' no further than the mines. Company's been advertising all way 'cross the country." She shook her head. "I've got no call to hire anyone, even though my husband's in the bullpen. What business there is, I can handle myself."

"Well, I thank you, ma'am," said Mick. "Let me know if things change and you need help."

Mrs. Graves clucked her tongue, and her brows came together in a V across her forehead. "Things is in a bad way, and I know ya lost yer ma. I'd help ya if I could."

Mick tried the dry-goods store next, then the dairy, the saloons, and finally the sawmill. It was the same story everywhere. The only paying work in town was underground. It was dark when he trudged home, still not ready to consider that option. But that night in bed, unable to sleep, he could no longer ignore the decision that lay before him.

The only way to keep a roof over his family's head, the only way to earn money to feed them, was to work in the mines. He feared the dark tunnels like death itself. The miners returning to the surface day after day—*if they were lucky*—were like condemned men. They emerged covered with gray dust from head to toe. If they weren't blown up or buried alive, they would die slowly, coughing themselves into the grave.

Maybe he could do it for a short time, just until Da got free. The army couldn't hold him long. He was innocent. 'Course, Mick would have to apply for the work permit. He'd have to swear off the union. Could he betray all that his father stood for? He twisted in bed, his thoughts burning like a fever.

Sometime after midnight, Moira's thin wail cut through his torment. Bridey didn't rouse, so he went down the ladder to tend the baby. He picked her up from her basket by the stove, but she didn't stop crying. She bawled louder and louder while he waited for a tin cup of milk to warm on the stove. Bouncing, jiggling, cuddling—nothing quieted her.

"There . . . there . . ." he whispered. "Shh, little Moira, shh." He stirred a dollop of corn syrup into the warm milk and began to spoon the mixture into her tiny red mouth, as he had seen Bridey do earlier. He felt awkward, and feared he spilled more down her neck than down her throat. But she stopped her noise, and in time seemed to grow satisfied. Lying still between spoonfuls, she looked up at him with her round black eyes. When she would swallow no more, he put her back in the basket. But she would have none of it and started to squall again.

He picked her up. "Hey, Moira. Don't cry," he whispered, holding her to his chest and rocking her. "Go to sleep now."

But the baby was wide awake, and everytime Mick put her down, she wailed. So he sat by the stove and held her.

"My, you're a strong little one," he told her as she kicked her legs. He had to keep rewrapping the blanket. Marveling at her tiny fingers, he let her grab on to his thumb, which she gripped and wouldn't let go of. An unfamiliar feeling came over him. It was nice, like when Mr. Delaney complimented him. But there was something about it that hurt, an ache deep in his chest.

Moira pulled his thumb into her mouth and fell asleep sucking. Watching her, he knew that, whatever it took, he had to do what his mother had asked. He must take care of his brother and sisters.

The next morning Mick joined the men gathered in front of the bank. The line moved quickly, and he soon stood in the lobby. Snipes's voice lay in the air like slime on still water. From where he stood behind a dozen men, Mick couldn't see Burbidge's assistant, but he could hear his patter.

"You're doing the right thing," said Snipes. "The union's dead, and high time. Those good-fer-nothing, murdering thieves are all locked up where they belong."

Mick's head ached as he watched one miner after another stoop at the small table in front of Snipes, put his right hand on the Bible, and answer the company man's questions.

Then it was his turn.

"Ah! Young Shea, you've seen the light, have you? Maybe I'll get my rent money, after all."

Mick's face flamed. He doubled his fists and took a step toward the little man.

"Hit me, will you?" Snipes drawled, his flabby white face rounding into a smile. "I thought you'd come looking to work in the mines like these honest men." He waved an arm.

Mick struggled for control, his temples throbbing.

"You're just a troublemaker," said Snipes.

A hand clasped Mick by the elbow. "Easy, son." He didn't recognize the whiskered face of the miner holding him back, but the firm grip and kindly tone brought him to himself, reminded him what he had to do. He bit his tongue and opened his clenched fists. The oily laugh that rolled up from Snipes's shaking belly didn't touch him. He looked straight into the man's eyes and steeled himself. "You need men to work your mine. I'm here to apply for the job."

Deflated slightly, Snipes nodded toward the Bible. "We'll give you a chance."

Mick placed his hand on the smooth leather of the holy book.

"Do you solemnly swear to tell the truth, the whole truth, and nothing but the truth?"

"I do."

"Have you ever been a member of the Western Federation of Miners, or any miners' union?"

"No."

"Have you ever participated in any union activity against a mine in this district?"

"No."

"Do you solemnly swear before God and those present you will not participate in any union activity, nor join, nor seek to join any union so long as you are employed in the Coeur d'Alene mining district?"

As he listened to Snipes drone through the questions, Mick felt sweat dampen his armpits and groin. He thought of Da, his passion for the union strangled in the bullpen.

"I do." Mick answered in a man's voice, but he felt like a kicked cur.

"Sign here."

The scratch of the fountain pen sounded loud in Mick's ears. It took an effort to finish his short signature. His hand ached when he laid down the pen.

"Report to the Bunker Hill at six tomorrow morning," said Snipes.

★ ★ ★

The next morning Mick woke early and couldn't get back to sleep. He dressed for the mine and went down to the kitchen. The house was quiet; even Moira slept soundly. Bridey had moved the baby's basket next to her own bed in her tiny room at the back of the house. Mick stoked up the fire and added a log, but still he shivered.

He had taken down two of Da's long-burning miner's

candles before going to bed. Now he went to the shelf by the door and picked up a third. Deep in the mine, he would depend on a single candle to see. It would be good to have some extras. He struck a match and tested one of the candles. The wick sputtered and went out. His fingers trembled as he struck another match and tried again. This time the flame took hold, burning the stearic, a mixture of hard fats. After a moment, he blew it out and put the candles in his pocket along with the metal candleholder.

He picked up Da's hat, the old one, misshapen and grimy from years of sweaty work underground, and put it on. Da's head was bigger, or maybe his hair just more bushy. The hat sat low on Mick's head.

Sitting down at the table, he nibbled at a cold biscuit, knowing he should eat. But he wasn't hungry.

"That's Da's hat." Mick twisted in his chair. He hadn't heard Nat coming down the ladder from the loft. The boy stood with his hands on his hips. "You got Da's hat and candles."

"Go back to sleep, Nat." Mick turned away, but Nat grabbed his shirtsleeve.

"Whatcha doin' with Da's mining gear?"

Mick stood and shook off his brother. "Da's not here. I'm the head of the family for now."

"That don't mean his stuff is yours."

"I'm just borrowing it."

Nat's voice had wakened Bridey, and she came out with her finger to her lips. "You'll wake Moira," she whispered.

Nat ignored his sister. He jumped and snatched at Da's hat. Mick clapped a hand to his head, pinning the hat in place.

125

"Lay off," he said. "I'm going to work in the Bunker Hill."

"You can't!" Nat shouted, lunging at Mick.

Mick held his little brother in a bear hug, trapping Nat's swinging arms to his sides. "You don't understand," he said, breathing hard. "I have to do it."

Nat struggled away. "Scab!"

The word tore into Mick's brain, burning a trail. He leapt for his brother, seized him by the throat of his shirt, and smashed a blow to his jaw. Nat's head pitched back, and he made a strangled noise in his throat. Mick felt the weight of him. "Stand up," he bellowed.

Nat found his feet and spat in Mick's face. "You're a low-down scab!" he shouted. "A shame on Da and all of us."

Mick hit him again. The boy sank to a heap on the floor.

Bridey ran and knelt next to him, but Nat stumbled to his feet and ran out the door.

Mick stood panting.

"You're just like them." It was Bridey confronting him now.

What the hell?

"You're just like Da, striking out at anybody weaker than you."

He turned away, but she got in his face. "Just like the soldiers."

Mick stared at her. "I'm not like that," he said.

"Yes, you are." She stamped her foot, and Mick's eyes crossed as they tried to focus on her wagging finger. "You're as bad as those rich mine owners taking advantage of people."

His hand shot out, and he slapped Bridey hard across the face.

126

The smack cracked between them like lightning. The room, the house, the world seemed to fall away. They were spinning, round and round. A loud rushing noise filled Mick's ears, but Bridey wasn't making a sound. He could see her lips clamped shut, her hands up to ward off further blows. A stain was growing on her cheek, a blood-red shadow in the shape of a hand.

The whirling slowed, and Mick turned away. He squeezed his eyes closed. He shook his head and managed to shut out the shock on Bridey's face but not the image burned in his brain. It was Da, his hand raised, advancing on Mam; Mick himself and Bridey hiding behind her skirts; Da swinging; the slap; the door slamming; Mam crying.

Mick shuddered. He grabbed his dinner pail from the table. Why had Bridey provoked him? Things were bad enough already. He was only trying to do what was best for the family. He couldn't believe that Bridey and Nat had criticized him. He left the house with Moira's shrill cries raw in his ears.

Fueled by his anger, Mick arrived at the Bunker Hill in a short time. In his mind he kept up the argument with Bridey and Nat, defending himself. He stopped short at the sight of the group of strikebreakers gathered near the entrance to the mine. About thirty men dressed in their diggers waited for the boss to give the word. A few jawed, their loud voices cutting the morning air. Most stood quietly, smoking or drinking coffee from the tin cups they carried with them.

Mick felt loath to join them, but he was one of them. He was a scab. A tremor passed through him. He wanted to run back down the gulch.

"Howdy, Mick."

Mick whirled around to see who had spoken. The man had come up behind him without a sound. How'd this lanky miner know his name?

"Ready for a day's work?" The man smiled slow, but his friendliness spread easily to his pale blue eyes, and he stretched out a hand to Mick.

Mick shook his hand. "Pleased to meet you, mister."

"Call me Hank. I was behind you signing on yesterday." Hank pumped his hand hard several times before letting go. His sandy blond hair and beard were clipped close. He didn't look young, but he wasn't as old as Da. Mick hadn't taken in the man's face yesterday, but he remembered the easy strength. "So your pa's in the bullpen?"

Mick avoided Hank's gaze, and when the shift whistle blew just then, he used the noise as an excuse to ignore him. He headed toward the men who were lining up at the open shaft.

Two steel tracks snaked out of the tunnel in the mountain. They led to the loading platform of the tramway. From deep in the mine where they worked, the men would use handcars to bring the ore to the surface. Each car could carry sixteen cubic feet of rock.

Because the mill had been blown up, no ore could be processed. But the tram was running, carrying the ore down the mountain to the railroad, where it would be shipped out to concentrators in Butte and Omaha.

Mick stood among the miners, most taller and broader than he, and felt a sense of dread. Could he handle the buzzy, the huge power drill that was run by compressed air?

Each packed a pressure of two hundred pounds to the square inch. He'd heard that a team could drill twenty holes per shift with a buzzy—ten times the work two men could do by hand. Mick lifted Da's hat and ran his fingers through his hair. He was born to this, he told himself. He could do it.

TWENTY

The darkness of the shaft closed in on Mick, squeezing his chest like a blacksmith's vise. Light bulbs hung at intervals from the roof of the tunnel cast hulking black shadows as the men walked forward. But the atmosphere was gloomy and the air humid. And Mick knew that the electric wire feeding the bulbs would eventually come to an end, and he and the others would depend solely on their candles to keep the blackness at bay.

Watching the shoulders of the man in front of him, he concentrated. Inhale . . . exhale. He began counting his steps as he walked on the planks that were laid between the steel rails: five, six, seven, . . . twenty, twenty-one, twenty-two. Down into the mine went the line of men, like a centipede crawling into the earth.

Mick had counted into the hundreds by the time they reached the end of the main tunnel and began to climb a ladder into a chamber above. Here several channels branched off in drifts that followed veins of ore, or crosscut tunnels that bisected the ore body. Mick continued to follow close on the heels of the miner in front of him. When they reached the stopes, the enlarged areas where the actual drilling took place, the smell of the recent dynamite blasts filled Mick's nose. Dust from the explosions had settled, but the miners' footsteps kicked it up in little puffs. Fine as flour, the pale gray particles formed a veil in the flickering light of the candles. Mick fought the urge to hold his breath, to close his nose to the very dust that had clogged Da's lungs and caused his hacking cough.

"Hey, greenhorn!" The shift boss's voice cut through Mick's fear. He was directing pairs of men to start work in each stope, and he motioned Mick ahead.

Mick heard Hank's voice at his elbow. "I'll take care of the young'un."

The boss nodded in agreement and left the two of them at a pile of muck that seemed to rise in the dim waver of Hank's candle. Hank searched the rock walls of the tunnel for a crevice. When he found one, he stuck in the steel prong of his candleholder, or Italian stiletto, as some miners called it. Mick had heard of fights that ended with a stab wound from a long sharp candleholder.

"Stand back. I'll bar down and we'll get started," said Hank. He grasped the end of a steel bar about three feet long and banged it hard on the ceiling of the tunnel, right over the pile of debris. A chunk of rock the size of Mick's head fell, along with a cascade of smaller rocks and dust.

By hitting again and again with the bar at different points overhead and on the sides of the stope, Hank brought down anything that was loose. Mick watched, realizing the importance of this job—barring down. It would keep loose rock from falling on them as they shoveled out the muck.

Each pair of shovelers had a wheelbarrow, and Mick

trundled theirs near the pile of debris. He and Hank began to shovel.

When they had a full load, one of them would wheel it along the tunnel to the chute and dump it. Below, an ore car waited on rails to carry it to the surface.

The work required all of Mick's strength but not much thought. In his mind he replayed that morning's argument with his sister and brother, getting mad all over again as he remembered the way they had spoken to him.

"Hey, slow down," said Hank. "Shoveling so wild like that, you'll never last the shift."

Mick paused and leaned on his shovel. He wiped the sweat from his face on his shirtsleeve.

"Pace yourself," Hank said. "Here, borrow my gloves. Your hands'll be like raw meat." He pulled off the worn leather gloves and held them toward Mick.

"No, thanks." Mick thrust his shovel into the heap of rock and threw another scoop into the wheelbarrow. He didn't need pity.

Dust thickened the air; the candle cast ghostly shadows. Mick shifted his thoughts to Moira. She was why he was here in this dark hellhole. Mam had asked him to care for her, and he would. Why couldn't Nat and Bridey appreciate what he was doing, how much he was giving up for them?

He thought of the college in Spokane—Gonzaga College. He pictured himself sitting in a classroom, listening to a black-robed teacher. Shelves of books lined the walls of the room, books filled with information of every kind. Reading those books, studying under the Jesuit fathers—surely he'd find his way beyond the bloody mud of labor war, beyond the helpless crying of a motherless baby.

Time dragged. Mick found that if he focused on thoughts of someday going to college, he could keep his aching arms working. When word came for the noon dinner break, Mick tossed down his shovel and sprawled on the ground against the wall of the tunnel. Opening his dinner bucket, he tore at the bread he'd carried from home. He gulped from the water dipper when it came around.

Hank sat down next to him.

"I'm guessing you ain't done much mining," he said in his slow, easy way. He scratched his beard and burped. "No sin in that. A body's got to start sometime. Now me, I come from a long line of mining stock." He leaned close to Mick and whispered, "Me and my brothers—*union*, all the way." He held up a clenched fist, then dropped it. "Broke me heart to sign those papers." He sounded as if he were mourning his one true love.

"Then why are you here?" Mick asked.

"Shh!" Hank stood up just as the shift boss came into view around the corner. "We're up an' at it."

"Better be," said the company man, giving Mick a hard look. "I'll have no sluggards."

Mick got to his feet, every muscle screaming in protest. He tried not to look at his bleeding hands as he picked up his shovel. Why had he been so darned stubborn about Hank's gloves? He glanced up. Hank had not started work. He stood holding out the gloves to Mick.

Mick took them. "Hank, I'll get you a new pair soon as I get my first paycheck."

"No, you won't. And don't argue with me."

Mick grinned. Maybe he could make it till the whistle blew. Maybe.

The grueling work went on. He and Hank finished shoveling all the muck left by the previous shift's blasts. Then it was time to start drilling holes for the next round of dynamite.

They placed a steel arm across the shaft and jackscrewed it tight. Together they lifted the machine drill and mounted it on the arm. Miners called the buzzy the widow maker. Mick had heard plenty of stories about it. He knew it had a tendency to loosen rock from the ceiling during drilling. He stood back, fighting panic while Hank took the first turn.

The deafening barrage of the drill in his ears sank into his flesh and bones, numbing him. He cleared away rubble as Hank drilled a pattern of holes into the rock above their heads. When they finished, an explosives man would come and fill the holes with sticks of dynamite. After lighting the fuses, he'd run to safety yelling a warning, *"Fire in the hole!"* The resulting explosion would rock the entire mine. It could bring down six tons of rock. Each cycle of drilling, dynamiting, and clearing away debris, pushed the drift, or tunnel, about three feet farther.

Mick's turn on the drill was short. The throbbing power of the machine nearly shook his arms from their sockets. The force of hard rock opposing the blistering bit reverberated through him like the burst of a hundred rifle shots. The drill trailed two long hoses that supplied air and water. Compressed air powered the drill, and a fine spray of water cooled and lubricated the whirling bit. The water was meant to dampen the flying dust as well, but it did little in that respect. Mick was soon sweating, exhausted, and fighting for breath. After managing to drill one hole, he went back to mucking.

As the hours crept by, the endless rhythm of shoveling beat upon his brain. Something deep inside him began to give way. Maybe it was Hank's kindness, or maybe the work that exhausted every part of him left no energy for anger. Whatever the reason, Mick began to register the shock and pain he'd seen in Bridey's eyes. *He'd struck her.* The shame of it inched through him. He wanted to blame her. But as his shovel blade scraped solid rock, he knew he was up against something undeniable as well. Bridey had spoken the truth. He was no better than Da.

TWENTY-ONE

As they emerged from the mine at quitting time, Mick's shoulders sagged. His arms were numb. He wanted to lie down on the spot and not budge for days.

"Good job," Hank said when they were on the rutted road down the gulch. "You'll make a miner, all right."

Mick flushed, surprised at how proud he felt at the miner's compliment. "You've been mighty kind, Hank. You worked more than your share. I owe you."

"Naw, you and me, we're pardners."

A lump swelled so big in Mick's chest he couldn't speak for a few moments. He thought of the words Hank had said at noon. What had brought him to the Coeur d'Alenes in this troubled time? Shirtsleeves now hid the tattoo on his shoulder, but Mick had seen the crossed sledges with the pick and shovel when Hank stripped down during his turn at the buzzy.

"Hank, why'd you sign on?" he asked. "Why'd you break faith with the union?"

Hank acted as though he hadn't heard the questions. He kept walking, his eyes fixed on something distant. Mick feared he had pressed the miner's goodwill too far. Then Hank turned a sharp look on him.

"Boy, I'm a union man till I die. This here's temporary." His voice took on a gruff, fierce quality. "Sometimes you gotta do what you gotta do. Harry, that's my brother, his lungs just plugged up and he couldn't get no air in 'em. Died just like me pa. Left his wife an' four young'uns. I gotta take care of 'em, and my own wife an' kids, too."

It was as if a dam had burst. The words just came streaming out. Mick felt the conflicting emotions under the words, and his sense of kinship with the man grew. They came around a turn and could see the town spread out below. The army camp on the flats to the west, the bullpen, and a Northern Pacific train pulling into the depot, its whistle splitting the evening air.

"This is a good wage." A defiant note had crept into Hank's tone. "It's a dollar a day more than a man makes in the eastern coalfields."

Mick nodded. They had reached McKinley Street. He held out his hand. "I don't know how to thank you," he said.

"You just come back in the morning." Hank's grip was light, mindful of Mick's sores. His face carried a solemn look. "You'll do fine."

Mick turned up Main Street, dragging his feet. He didn't want to face Bridey, didn't want to admit that what he'd done was wrong. But he knew he had to.

The sizzle of bacon met him as he opened the door. Something else, too—*aha!* Beans baked with tomatoes and molasses. Where had his sister gotten all this food? Bridey pulled a pan of cornbread from the stove as he came in. She put the pan down on a trivet on the table and turned and faced him.

"Bridey—"

She interrupted him. "Mick, I've cooked a grand supper. But it doesn't mean I'm not angry. It was wrong for you to strike me. I won't have it."

With her shoulders rigid and her voice fierce, she looked like a bantam rooster set to fight. Mick went to her. He took her hands in his. "Bridey, I'm sorry. I won't hit you again."

Her eyes welled with tears. "I never thought you'd be like Da."

Mick turned away, the heat of shame rising to his cheeks. "I don't want to be."

A shaft of late sunlight coming in the west window illuminated a swirl of mine dust that had risen from his diggers. He hung his head. No, he'd never wanted to be like Da.

Bridey touched his elbow. "Go wash up."

He went out the kitchen door to the pump, removed his shirt, and doused his head under the gushing water. Soaping up, he scrubbed his skin with the pig-bristle brush— scrubbed until long after the grime of the day's work had been washed away.

"Supper's ready," Bridey called from the doorway. Mick remembered the mysterious meal laid out in the kitchen. He was starving. Shaking water from his hair, he took the towel and fresh shirt she handed him.

"The union in Spokane sent a whole trainload of food," Bridey said as he came inside. "It's for the families of the men in the bullpen. All I had to do was go down to the union hall. They looked up Da's name on the list and gave me all the vittles I could carry."

His mouth was watering. He stared at the pot of beans

and the plate of bacon. Steam rose from the cornbread, and he drew in the tempting smells. He hadn't eaten food like this since . . . since before all this trouble had started. He was so hungry, and yet he could not eat union food. He didn't *deserve* to eat it.

The grit of mine dust filled his mouth, the ache of drilling and shoveling overwhelmed his muscles. Sinking into a chair, Mick held his head in his hands.

Bridey seemed to read his mind. "Eat," she said. Mick looked up, surprised at the sharpness in her voice. "I'll have no nonsense in this house," she told him as she cut a piece of cornbread, sliced it in two on a plate, and ladled beans over it. "Go ahead," she commanded again, piling bacon on and setting the food in front of him.

He was too tired to argue.

"Where's Nat?" he asked when his plate was clean. Bridey served him another helping.

"He's not so quick to forgive," she said, avoiding his gaze.

Anger flashed through Mick. "He help you today?"

"He filled the woodbin; he even tended Moira."

"Where's he now?"

"He said he won't be in the same house with you."

Mick let his fork fall to the plate with a clatter. He pushed back his chair and stood up. "You tell that scamp . . . tell him . . ." He grasped the straight-back chair and slammed it into place under the table.

"Mick, don't." Bridey pinned him with a cold stare.

He felt the blood charge to his head. His fists tensed, and he fought to keep his temper from exploding. It was like fire inside him, bursting to get out. He spun away from his sister, folded his arms across his chest, and sucked air into his lungs. Then bit by bit, he felt his fury drain away. He must not think about Nat right now. He had a job to do, and it would take all his strength.

Rousing his exhausted muscles, he climbed the ladder to the loft. He fell asleep on the ticking without even undressing.

TWENTY-TWO

"**H**alf a dozen miners escaped from the bullpen last night," Bridey announced as Mick shed his work clothes by the door. Caked with dust that sweat had turned to mud, they practically stood up by themselves.

His second day in the mine, every move he made had caused an ache or a pain somewhere. He felt as if he'd been dragged backward through a knothole. Now at the end of a third day of shoveling and drilling, his body had gone numb. He was completely worn out. He pulled on his flannel long johns and sank down at the supper table without washing up.

"The miners bribed a soldier to help them." Bridey paused in the middle of dishing up a plate of boiled vegetables and side pork. "He let them out of the stockade. And, Mick, you won't believe this"—she waved the plate half filled with food in one hand and the big wooden spoon in the other—"a group of officers got dead drunk. They didn't even know it when the miners stripped off their uniforms. Dressed up in army uniforms, the miners just got on the train and rode to Thompson Falls."

"Bridey, can I have my supper?"

"Isn't that a great story?" she asked. She dipped into

the kettle for another spoonful of stew, then set the plate in front of him. "You know what else? The railroad's running a passenger train down from Burke and Gem every day. It's packed with folks coming to see their men in the bullpen."

Mick grunted and dug into his stew. He didn't speak until he'd eaten every bite. "Any news about Da?"

"Nat's talking to him through the fence every day. He's got a bunk to sleep in now, and he's well." Bridey grimaced. "Some of the men are real sick, though."

Moira had wakened and begun to cry. Bridey sat near the stove feeding her. Mick watched as she expertly spooned milk into the baby's hungry mouth. She was keeping Moira alive. Not only that, but cooking for the family and sending food and clean clothes to Da in the bullpen. She was working almost as hard as he was.

"How's Nat?" he asked.

Bridey put Moira to her shoulder and stood, patting the baby's tiny back to encourage a burp.

"You're too hard on Nat," she said. "He's barely out of knickers. He's lost Mam . . . and Da's in that horrible jail." Her lip trembled.

Mick got up, groaning at the stiffness in his legs, and put his arms around both her and Moira. She leaned on his shoulder and wept.

"I'm so scared," she said through her tears. "The union men are marching around the bullpen with sticks they pretend are guns. The soldiers are drinking in the saloons, and your Mr. Delaney is publishing newspaper editorials stirring everybody up."

"What's he writing?"

Moira whimpered.

"Read for yourself," answered Bridey. "I've got to change the baby's nappy." She pointed to the newspaper on top of the woodbin.

Picking it up, Mick gulped back a swell of longing. He remembered his days working at the *Bugle* like another lifetime. He skimmed the headlines, then went right to Mr. Delaney's editorial.

CONDITIONS IN BULLPEN
"CRUEL, UNUSUAL"
by Patrick Delaney

This editor calls on the United States Congress to investigate the situation here in the Coeur d'Alene Mining District.

Men denied their rightful habeas corpus proceedings are confined in conditions not fit for man or beast.

Greed and exploitation rule as government "of the people, by the people and for the people" is subverted by politicians in cahoots with wealthy industrialists.

This editor urges every good citizen of the district to voice his outrage at the present course of events by using peaceful but determined means.

Mick agreed with Mr. Delaney, but he had other problems to think about. The back rent his family owed, for one thing. Working at the Bunker Hill for three dollars a day, it would take him nearly two months to earn the money. Could he keep it up that long?

★ ★ ★

By the end of his second week in the mine, Mick began to believe that he might last. The work exhausted him—when he wasn't working or eating, he slept—but he was learning fast. And his body had become more flexible, his muscles solid.

"You're young," said Hank, pinching Mick's biceps. "This work just makes you stronger." He shook his head. "At my age, it's a different story."

The shift had knocked off an hour early on account of the weekend, and they were walking down the gulch. Mick kept touching the bills folded in his pocket—thirty-six dollars—his first two weeks' wages.

"Wanna have a whiskey on me at the Iron Horse?" asked Hank. "We oughta celebrate."

Mick shook his head. "I may be a miner now, but I won't pass muster with the bartender, I know that."

Hank laughed and clapped him on the shoulder. "When you can stand at the bar, you'll owe me a drink. Hey, pard?"

"You bet, pardner." Mick smiled at his friend and waved as he turned up McKinley Street toward home. Fingering the money in his pocket, he pulled into his lungs the scent of the fresh spring grasses that had turned the valley a brilliant green. The day had been warm, a hint that summer might be near. Mick felt a certain pride, not only because he was bringing home money for the family but also because of the work he had done. For the first time, he understood Da's satisfaction in pitting muscle and machine against

144

mountain. The work demanded the full measure of a man, and he felt proud to have been tested and to have not failed. The roofs of the town reflected the rosy glow of the setting sun, and Mick felt a similar warmth wash over him. He quickened his step, then ran the last few strides.

Holding the cash in his hand, Mick flung open the door, ready to dance a jig with Bridey. But he stopped, shocked at what he saw. Nat sat on a stool in the middle of the room. He was loading a shiny pistol. Mick hadn't seen his brother since the morning he'd started work at the mine. He looked small, his face dirty as an orphan's, the gun huge in his hands.

A log shifted in the stove with a thump, followed by the snap of sparks. Nat scowled.

"Give me the gun," Mick said, stuffing the money into his pocket.

"No. I won't do nothing you say."

Mick took a step closer. Nat thrust the gun behind his back.

"Where'd you get a gun? And where's Bridey and Moira?"

"They've gone to Mrs. Bielaski's for milk." Nat tossed his head in defiance, ignoring Mick's first question. "Mick, you can't stop me. I'm going to help Da escape. Anton and I've got it all worked out."

"You've got a plan? Why don't you tell me about it?"

Nat shook his head. "I won't talk with a scab. You're enemy, just like those soldiers." He jumped from the stool and edged toward the door.

Mick blocked his way. "I need to tell you something important."

"No!" said Nat, and he brought the gun around in front of him and pointed it at Mick.

A stab of sadness wrenched through Mick. The brave look on Nat's face almost hid the scared little boy.

"Nat, I was wrong," he said. "I never should have hit you." He leaned forward, offering his hands to his brother. "Can you forgive me?"

Nat dropped his fierce mask. He looked ready to burst into tears. The gun wavered, but he strengthened his grip and steadied it. "You signed those papers against the union. You're a traitor. You don't even care about Da."

"I want him home as much as you do," said Mick. "How are you thinking to do it?"

"Anton got the guns. One for Da and one for Mr. Scheffer. Each has six rounds. We're putting them inside loaves of bread." He tipped his head to the fresh loaf sitting on the table. "The soldiers let us bring food once a day. Tonight Da and Mr. Scheffer will have the loaded pistols."

"That's crazy." Mick threw up his hands. "Da won't let you do that!"

"Da won't know till he eats the bread. But Anton's got the plan all set. They'll shoot their way out and take the trail over the mountains to Thompson Falls."

Mick shook his head. He couldn't believe what Nat was telling him. "They'll be killed, for sure. There's a whole company standing guard."

"Better to die fighting than to sit in a pen like an animal—that's what Anton says."

With a lightning swipe, Mick tore the gun from Nat's

hands. Nat screamed and grappled with him, trying to get the pistol back. Mick held it high over his head as Nat pummeled him.

"That's my gun!" yelled Nat. "Gimme it."

The door slammed, and Bridey came in with the baby, who was screaming nearly as loud as Nat. Bridey drew back in surprise, clutching Moira in one arm and a full milk jar in the other.

"What's going on?" she cried. "Mam wouldn't allow a gun in this house, and neither will I."

The expression on Bridey's face looked just like Mam's when she scolded them. The tone of her voice even quieted the baby. Mick felt like a small boy caught drinking the molasses. "It—it's Nat's," he said.

"Nat's?" Bridey glared from one to the other and raised an eyebrow. She put the milk down and held out her hand. "Give it here."

Mick handed it to her, and she stuck it in the bodice of her apron. "Mick, I've got bad news," she said. "The soldiers have arrested Mr. Delaney. They've thrown him in the bullpen, and they've confiscated his printing press."

"What?" said Mick. "They can't—"

"They can and they did. Both of you"—she motioned to Nat and Mick—"go out and chop me some kindling. Fill the woodbin and build up the fire for cooking supper. I have to feed this baby."

Mick's last bit of strength crumpled. Only the force of Bridey's command carried him outside to the woodpile. Nat followed and plopped down on the chopping block. Mick leaned against the stacked cedar. His mind was a mess of images swirling like leaves in a gust of wind. He was too tired to get hold of any sense.

With a pang he remembered working in the newspaper office with Mr. Delaney, coming home to supper with his family, his mam laughing, even Da going on a tirade during the family meal—he missed it all. For, he realized now, things would never go back to the way they had been.

The sound of a sniffle broke through his weariness. Nat was crying, tears and snot clearing tracks through the grime on his face. Mick wished he were eight years old and could give in to tears, too. For it hurt that bad, thinking of Mr. Delaney and Da in the stockade, and Mam . . . Mam in the grave. He knelt down and put his arms around the boy.

"Oh, Nat, everything'll work out," he said.

Nat stiffened and pulled away, but Mick hugged him close. "We'll rescue Da," he said. "Somehow we'll do it." After a moment he felt his brother relax against him, sobbing. Mick held him, patting his dirty matted hair.

Nat lifted his head. "You smell like Da."

"It's the dust," said Mick. "I'm a miner now." He pulled his little brother to his feet. "We better get to work, or that Bridey'll be out here after us. Better yet, I'll chop the kindling, you run tell Anton his scheme's a bust."

Nat hesitated, but Mick gave him a little nudge. "Go on now. You're having no part of that plan. Tell him, and get back here in time for supper."

★ ★ ★

When they finished eating and the work was done, they all sat in front of the stove. For a spell there was no sound but

148

the crackle of the fire and the creak of the rocker where Bridey sat with Moira.

"Why don't you read a bit?" she said, just in the way Mam used to.

Mick didn't want to, but he got up and left the warmth of the stove and went into the bedroom where his mother had died. Light from the doorway shone on the dresser. There on top of an embroidered cloth lay Mam's Bible. He paused, superstitious about touching it. Giving himself a mental shake, he picked the heavy book up. He was glad to return to the fire and the company of his brother and sisters.

A black satin ribbon marked the spot where Mam had left off in the Book of Judith.

"And she washed her body, and anointed herself with the best ointment, and plaited the hair of her head . . ."

Mick read aloud how Judith put on her finest clothing and sandals, adorned herself with bracelets, earrings, and rings, and made herself so lovely no man could resist her.

He read through Judith's foray into the Assyrian camp and her return to the besieged city of Bathulia with the head of General Holefernes in her leather pouch. Then the words blurred, and his voice began to drift off. His eyes closed, and his chin fell to his chest. Bridey nudged him awake, and they all went to bed.

But it was that reading, the story of Judith, that sparked the dream. And when Mick woke the next morning, he knew how they would spring Da from the stockade.

TWENTY-THREE

"That's silly," Nat said when he heard Mick's plan.

"It *is* silly—but that's why it'll work," said Mick. "Do you really want Da shooting it out with a whole company of soldiers?"

Nat bit his lip and thought about it. They were seated around the table in the kitchen, eating bacon, eggs, and flapjacks after returning from Sunday mass. Ever since he awoke, Mick's mind had been off and running with the notion of jumping Da and Mr. Delaney from the bullpen.

Bridey reached over and put her arm around Nat. "Mam wouldn't want Da in a gunfight with the soldiers," she said.

The boy frowned and crossed his arms over his chest.

"We'll do it tonight," said Mick.

"Tonight? But we've barely had time to think about it," said Bridey.

"Hank told me the mines in the Slocan District in British Columbia are hiring union men." Mick spoke even though his mouth was full. "We'll have to leave town right away. I figure that's the place to go."

"Leave?" Bridey's voice was shrill. "But this is our home. And Mam . . . Mam's . . ." She paused and strangled a sob. "Mam's here," she finished.

"Da will be a fugitive. It won't be safe to stay."

Nat had been tucking into his flapjacks, but now he paused. "What d'ya think Da's going to say when he finds out you're a scab?" he said, glowering at Mick.

Mick scowled back at him.

"But we'll have to pack everything. . . ." Bridey slumped in her seat.

"No," said Mick. "We can't take much. We'll have to walk at least as far as Spokane. The soldiers will be watching the train and livery wagons."

Bridey started to weep, covering her face with her apron.

Mick patted her. "Mam would understand that we have to leave," he said.

Nat pushed a piece of bacon around on his plate. He had lost his last bit of bluster.

A sudden weight of despair fell over Mick. He looked from Bridey to Nat and shook his head. They were just children. Then, closing his eyes, he willed himself to be strong. His family depended on him. That was all there was to it.

"Bridey . . . Nat," he said. "We can do this. We have to. There's no other way."

"But with the baby . . . And what about Da? Will he be in any shape to walk?" Bridey wheezed and wiped her eyes, but the tears kept coming. "How many days will it take us?"

"Da's strong. He can walk," said Nat. "Well . . . he might have to stop when he's coughing."

Mick nodded. "We can make it to Spokane in three days, even if we take it easy," he said. "We'll bring only what we can carry. Moira will be fine." He smiled. "She'll probably sleep the whole way.

"Come on," he said, standing up. "There's lots of work to do, and I can't manage it alone."

They went through the house, top to bottom, gathering supplies they would need for the trip and possessions they couldn't bear to leave behind. The pile on the table grew to overflowing, and they went through it all again. Mick flipped through the pages of *The Three Musketeers*, a gift from Mr. Delaney. He loved the book but chose instead to bring Mam's Bible. Nat decided on a tiny wooden soldier and returned the rest of the toys to the box he kept in a corner of the loft. Bridey clasped the china sugar bowl to her chest, then tucked it away on the shelf in the kitchen. Mick hated to think Snipes would take whatever was left. It would more than cover the rent, and right now he had more important worries.

Using their woolen blankets, they made packs, wrapping up extra clothing for themselves and Da. Mick packed the cast-iron skillet, coffeepot, matches, tin plates and cups, knives, and forks. From the pantry, they took cornmeal, potatoes, dried beans, coffee, two tins of tomatoes, and some dried apricots and plums.

"The packs will be heavy," said Mick. "But as we eat, they'll get lighter."

"We need cans of Eagle milk for Moira," said Bridey heading back to the pantry. "Luckily, these came in on the train with the goods donated by the Spokane union."

By early afternoon they were ready. Mick sent Nat to tell Da and Mr. Delaney their plan. "Be careful," he said.

"You may not be able to explain everything without being overheard. Just tell them to be ready to make a run for it tonight."

"What about Mr. Scheffer?" asked Nat.

"The more men involved, the riskier it'll be."

Nat started to argue, but Mick held up a hand. "Don't worry about Mr. Scheffer. Anton will find a way to help his da."

Mick wished he could say goodbye to Hank. But he couldn't spare the time to visit the boarding house. He hoped Hank would understand.

One last time, he walked through the rooms of the house where he had lived most of his life. The white curtains at the kitchen window ruffled in the afternoon breeze, brushing over the pots and pans where they hung on the wall in their usual places. It seemed as if any minute Mam would walk in and start peeling potatoes for supper. An ache filled his throat and threatened to bring tears to his eyes.

He hid his face from Bridey and lifted two of the readied bundles. "I'll go stash the packs," he mumbled and went out to the woodshed. There he added the ax to his load and set off toward the woods.

A short way into the trees, he took a path that wound along a little stream. It was perfect May weather, hot where the sun slanted through the pines, cool in the shade where the trees grew dense. A carpet of wild strawberries bloomed in each little clearing, and the spicy scent of warm ponderosa and fir needles filled the air.

It didn't take him long to reach the old prospector's cabin. Da had often brought them there to play on Sunday afternoons just like this one. The tiny shack smelled of rotting wood, but it would serve as a temporary shelter and rendezvous. Pale light sifted through the cracks in the walls and roof. Mick felt for a dry spot in a corner and dropped the packs. Then he headed back to get the second load. When he finished, it was late in the afternoon. He returned to the house. It was time to go over the strategy with Nat and Bridey one last time.

"All I do is bring food," said Nat. "Why can't I do something more exciting?"

"Your part is very important," said Mick. "The soldiers are used to you coming to see Da. Just remember, act calm. Don't do anything out of the ordinary."

"Except pinch Moira."

They all laughed.

"Not too hard," said Bridey, snuggling her face against the little blanket-wrapped infant on her shoulder.

"She'll be fine," said Mick. "Bridey? You know what to do?"

"Yes."

"Good. We'll meet when it's dark, in about an hour, behind the Carlton Hotel, near the officers' quarters."

The western sky blazed pink and orange as Mick set out toward Main Street. His stomach felt like a nest of moths all fluttering in fright. Knots of men stood along the street. They smoked and talked, bursting into occasional laughter. Music and voices spilled out into the evening from the Iron Horse and Royal Galena saloons. Only a couple of wagons rolled by, harnesses jingling. Sunday was the quietest evening in a mining town.

Mick was relieved that no one took any notice of him. He turned into the alley and stepped around to the back of the Royal Galena. A bulb glowed above the door that led to the rear stairs. Mick peered over his shoulder, looking up and down the alley. There was no one in sight. He took a deep breath and turned the knob. The well-oiled hinges opened without a sound. He kept his eyes on the toes of his work boots as he climbed toward the landing on the second floor.

Though covered with worn carpet, each step creaked loudly. Mick feared that every man in the street could hear him going up the stairs. When he reached the top, he felt winded. He stole a look about the landing, seeing only a sofa against the wall and a small round table next to it holding a lamp that lit the space with a golden shine.

A short, plump woman came down the hallway and greeted him. She was dressed in a bright green gown, which was cut low, her bosom rising from it like a full moon over the crest of the mountains. Mick looked down at his feet.

"A bit young, aren't you?" The woman's voice, low and musical, drew Mick's attention to her bright red lips. "You'd be a disappointment to me if I was your ma."

That sparked Mick's anger, but he held it in check, pushed it down. This woman wasn't fit for his mam to wipe her shoes on.

"I would like to speak to Miss Beatrice," he said.

The woman directed him to sit on the soft cushions of the sofa. She settled a broad smile upon him and patted his knee. "Let me see your money, then."

"I just want to talk—"

The smile disappeared. "There's nothing here for free," she said, "not even talk." Her voice was now as musical as a mule's bray, and she grabbed him by the jacket and, despite her size, jerked him to his feet.

"You don't understand." Mick shook himself free.

"Oh, I understand all right. Now, get on out of here, or I'll call Jake." She pointed a fierce finger to the door. "He'll horsewhip you."

Mick wanted to go. He'd just as soon turn and run down the stairs to the street and never see this place again. But he couldn't. He needed Miss Beatrice. His pay from the mine was in his pocket. He'd hoped to save it for the trip. But if his plan didn't work, there would be no trip at all. "I've got money."

"I oughta run you out of here." The woman's voice still sounded harsh, but she had moved back toward him, her eyes gleaming as she watched him pull out his money.

When she saw the greenbacks, she turned sharply. "Beatrice!" she called.

One of the doors halfway down the narrow corridor opened, and Miss Beatrice Beaufontaine stepped into the hall. Her eyes widened when she saw Mick.

"Go ahead, then," said the round woman, her voice again a soft melody.

"This *is* a surprise," said Miss Beatrice, sweeping out her hand to welcome Mick. He avoided her look and hurried into her room.

"It's not . . . ah . . . ah . . . a social call," Mick said, his palms sweating as the door clicked shut, enclosing them in the small bedroom. Only a bed and a chest of drawers holding a basin and pitcher furnished the room. A gilded mirror hung on one wall next to a peg draped with several brightly colored gowns. A heavy, sweet scent made him feel sick to his stomach.

"I need your help," he said. "I'll pay you."

"How much?"

"Ten dollars."

"Talk away. I'm listening." She sat down on the bed, inspecting her red-colored nails, first one hand, then the other, as Mick told her his idea.

"Twenty dollars," she said when he finished.

Mick winced. "That's more'n a week's wages!"

"That's my price, and I'll want the money now."

Mick hesitated. Miss Beatrice stood up and went to the door.

"Wait—twenty . . . That's fine," Mick stammered. He pulled out the money and handed it to her. "But we need to go right now, before the men are sent to their bunks for the night."

"You go ahead," she said. "We shouldn't be seen together. I'll meet you in fifteen minutes in that little stand of trees east of the stockade entrance."

Surprised that he now felt calm, Mick left the Royal Galena and hurried along the alley to join up with Bridey and Nat. They were waiting in the shadows near the Carlton Hotel, just as he had instructed.

"All set," he said, holding a finger to his lips to still their questions. "Miss Beatrice agreed to help. She'll be here any minute."

He led them past the rear of the officers' quarters, a tent

as large as a house, staked at the end of the street. They could see the main gate of the bullpen, an easy stone's throw away. Two electric bulbs, hanging on wires above the gate, lit the area, but the glow didn't stretch far into the surrounding darkness.

"Ready?" Mick asked in a low voice, pulling Bridey and Nat close to him.

They nodded, and Moira opened her eyes and batted her tiny fists in the air. The three smothered their giggles, and Mick squeezed the hands of his sister and brother. They heard a swish of skirts as Miss Beatrice joined them. Mick introduced her and went over what they would do one last time. He looked at the circle of faces around him, pale in the darkness, eyes solemn. Sudden doubt besieged him. What if his plan didn't work? What if they were caught? What if the soldiers started firing? He thrust the fear from his mind. "Whatever happens," he reminded them, "go to the prospector's cabin. We'll meet there."

"Right," whispered Nat, who was starting to squirm and shuffle his feet. "Now, is it time to go?"

"It's time."

Bridey settled Moira on her chest, took Nat's hand, and walked out of the trees. They skirted the officers' quarters and approached the gate, where two soldiers stood guard.

"Who's there? Step into the light." Mick could hear the soldier clearly.

Bridey and Nat obeyed, and Mick heard Bridey answer. Only a word or two of her thin voice reached him, but he knew she was telling about Mam dying, about the baby who'd never seen her da. Nat held up the cold baked potatoes, the soda bread. Bridey should be asking for Mr. Delaney. She was supposed to tell the guards that he was the baby's godfather, that the baby was sickly, and that they mustn't risk her dying without receiving a blessing from the godfather.

Mick's throat constricted, and he felt weak with anxiety. The taller guard listened, then waved his hands, as if explaining something. Bridey spoke again and held Moira up. The soldier stepped back and put out his arm, as if to ward off the baby's illness.

The other guard walked over, holding his rifle in one hand. Mick shivered. The second soldier appeared to make a decision. He unlatched the gate and swung it open. Mick could see a small crowd of prisoners inside. A holler went up from the gathering, and Bridey and Nat slipped into the bullpen with the soldiers at their side.

"Now!" Mick said, but Miss Beatrice had already picked up her skirts and was moving toward the gate. He followed, careful to stay in the shadows. He could see Da's silhouette inside the stockade. Bridey ran over to their father, and they embraced.

"Why, hello, y'all. What a nice evening," Miss Beatrice said as she sashayed up with a gay wave of her hand. The taller guard had moved into the bullpen, while the second stood just inside at the open gate. He held his rifle diagonally across his chest with both hands. Miss Beatrice stepped up close to him.

"I just thought it was time I paid a visit here," she sang out.

"Miss!" yelled the soldier. "Stop." He reached out to

grab her, then hesitated, unsure of what to do. Mick watched Miss Beatrice move straight into the bullpen, opening the gate wider with a flick of her hip as she went.

Shouts and whistles erupted from the miners. Jostling, they surrounded Miss Beatrice.

"Miss, come outta there!" the soldier shouted.

"I'll just be a minute," said Miss Beatrice. Mick wished he could have gone in, too, but he was afraid the soldiers might recognize him. His gaze sifted through the hubbub for Bridey, Nat, and Da, and he found them at the edge of the crowd near the gate. *Now,* he thought. *Nat, make your move.*

As if on cue, the startled wail of a baby broke over the noise of the prisoners. Bridey thrust the crying Moira into the arms of the taller soldier, who stood frozen, holding the wriggling bundle out in front of him. Mick saw Da edging toward the unmanned gate.

The other guard, who had followed Miss Beatrice into the swarm of prisoners, had a hold on her wrist.

"Please, sir, let me go," she cried. "I only want to visit a bit with these poor men."

Kaboom! There was the crack of a gunshot. And all hell broke loose. Two additional soldiers had arrived. One of them must have fired. Men screamed, pushed, and shoved.

Where was Mr. Delaney? Forgetting the danger, Mick dashed to the timbers of the fence, searching the bedlam for the face of his friend. He was supposed to escape with Da in the confusion.

"Mick!" Mr. Delaney reached through the barricade toward him, and Mick's stomach lurched with disappointment. The editor was still captive. The guards started swinging the gate shut, yelling at the prisoners to fall back.

"I'm sorry," Mick whispered, grabbing his friend's outstretched hand.

"Don't worry. I'll get a lawyer." Mr. Delaney squeezed Mick's fingers. "Go see Conner Malott, my friend at the newspaper in Spokane. Tell him I sent you. He'll give you a job." Then the editor was swallowed up by the crowd.

Mick backed into the shadows and surveyed the situation. One soldier had Bridey, who was carrying Moira, in tow, and they were heading toward the officers' quarters. Another soldier followed, holding Miss Beatrice by the elbow.

"Let me go," Bridey cried. "I've done nothing, and this baby is sick."

Mick saw no sign of Da or Nat. Had they gotten away? Half a dozen more soldiers arrived, securing the bullpen once again. Mick could do nothing more.

TWENTY-FOUR

Slipping back into the trees, Mick studied the activity at the bullpen. If Da had escaped, the soldiers hadn't figured it out. The reinforcements split up, some entering the stockade and ushering the prisoners into their quarters, others doubling up the guard around the perimeter.

Bridey, carrying Moira, had disappeared into the officers' tent along with Miss Beatrice. Would they arrest a woman, a girl, and a baby? Surely not, thought Mick. But if they did, it would be all his fault. Why had he ever thought such a scheme would work?

The scene before him grew quiet. Mick could hear only a murmur of voices and the soft chorus of uncountable peepers singing in the spring night. Had he been waiting ten minutes? Half an hour? He couldn't gauge it. Rising from his crouch in the underbrush, he stretched his aching knees. Maybe he should creep up to the tent and try to hear what was going on. He had taken two steps in that direction when the flap at the front was lifted and Bridey came out, with Moira in her arms. The baby was wailing.

"Don't show up here again," an officer called after them, sticking his head out of the tent flap. "This is no place for a girl or a baby."

162

Bridey didn't look back. She hurried away up the street past the Carlton Hotel. Mick sagged in relief. Then he, too, made his getaway, taking the alley. He met Bridey at the edge of town.

"Mick!" She flung one arm around him, while the other hung on to Moira.

"Did Da get out?"

"I don't know. There was so much happening so fast, so much noise—" She smothered a sob. "I don't know what happened to Nat, either."

"Let's go," said Mick. "They'll be waiting for us at the cabin."

He tried to believe his own words, but as they trudged along the path to the prospector's cabin, his doubts grew. A half-moon had risen above the ridge of mountains to the east. As it climbed in the sky, a bank of clouds dimmed its light. They made slow progress until their eyes got used to the darkness of the woods. When they reached the cabin and pushed open the door to empty blackness, neither said a word.

Moira woke and fussed. Bridey felt around on the floor for the packs.

"Light a candle, Mick. I think she's hungry. I'm looking for the canned milk."

Mick struck a match and lit one of Da's stearic candles. He stuck the miner's candleholder in a crack near the door. Bridey found the milk and can opener.

"I hope she'll take it cold," she said.

Mick felt restless. He couldn't just sit and wait, so he went outside and paced back and forth in front of the cabin.

Several times he thought he heard footsteps coming up the trail, but it was just the wind moving through branches. A coyote howled. A far-off gunshot raised the hair on his arms. *Just a drunken miner*, he told himself. *Nothing to worry about.* Going back inside, he wrapped up the pack Bridey had undone to get the milk. He rearranged their provisions against the back wall.

When the cabin door creaked and fell open, Mick leapt in alarm. He hadn't heard footsteps, but someone was there outside in the dark. Who?

"Mick!" Da came through the door and pulled him into a huge hug, so hard he couldn't speak. He felt Da's rough beard on his cheek, smelled his sweat. Then his father held him at arm's length. "Lad, you've the look of a man about you."

"Da . . ." A stinging, prickly feeling spread through Mick's nose, and his chest felt tight. "Da, it's only been a couple weeks."

"Seems like a year." His father's voice grew husky. "I've missed you."

He turned to his daughter. "Ah, Bridey, my love. . . . And this must be Moira." As Da peered down at the sleeping baby Bridey held, his face took on a haggard look. He blinked his eyes furiously and gathered the two close to him. The room was as still as a stope after a dynamite blast. Then Mick heard a low moan. And Da began to shudder.

Nat had come in with Da, and now he let forth a howl and ran to encircle his arms around his father's leg.

Da steadied himself. "Your Mam . . . did she . . . was she hurtin' at the end?"

Bridey shook her head, tears streaming down her face.

Mick tried to tell Da how Mam had been at the last, but a huge painful gulp filled his throat. He couldn't get the words out.

Da took Moira from Bridey. The baby woke and looked up at him with her bright eyes. "You were right to name her after your mam," he said, holding her gently to his heart. "Moira was the finest woman God ever made." His voice was strong now, but his lashes gleamed with tears.

Mick couldn't bear to watch him. He turned and started fidgeting with the packs.

"Time to move out," said Da. "I don't think anybody's on our trail, but they'll be after us come morning, for sure." He helped Bridey sling Moira over her chest in the piece of muslin that she had brought for carrying the baby on the trip.

"Da, I've got to tell you something," said Mick. Unable to meet his father's eyes, Mick stared at the dirt floor. "I . . . I went to work at the Bunker Hill. I signed the work permit."

He braced himself for the torrent of anger sure to come. Da gripped him by the shoulders, his strong fingers biting into Mick's flesh. Mick still couldn't raise his head to look at him. The candle sputtered. Moira made a soft cooing sound.

"Mick only did it for us," said Bridey. "For Nat, Moira, and me."

"I told him he was a scab," Nat said, thrusting himself between Mick and Da. "I told him you'd be mad."

"I'm sorry, Da," said Mick, finally meeting his father's eyes. "I didn't want to do it, but I couldn't see any other way."

In the flickering light of the candle, Da cast a huge shadow on the wall. But his body drooped, and with his dirty clothes and uncombed hair, he looked like a beaten man.

"These are hard times." Da's voice was thick and slow. "I don't blame you, lad."

The guilt slipped from Mick's shoulders. But he felt hollow inside as he stood facing his father. This man who'd always been like a solid rock now seemed to need something to lean on.

"Da, I even took my turn with the buzzy," he said.

"I'd expect no less." Da clapped Mick on the back. "What d'ya think of her?"

"She's powerful."

Da chuckled. "Lad, I always knew you had it in you to be a miner." The pride that had begun to spread through Mick wilted. He groped for words as they all picked up their packs.

But it was Da who spoke first. "I figure we head overland to Fort Sherman, keeping to the woods, and then head north to British Columbia," said Da. "The trusts ain't running things up there. A man can still do some prospecting."

Mick felt as if he couldn't get air, as if he was back in the dark of the mineshaft with the walls of the tunnel closing in.

Da held up a clenched fist, the union sign. "Here we come," he said. "We'll be mates, huh, Mick?" He pushed the door open and ushered Bridey and Nat out. Then he followed.

"No, Da. I'm not going to be a miner."

Da stopped, frozen for a moment with his back to Mick. "You'll do as I say," he said.

"I won't." Mick knew it was he who said those words, but it was a new self he didn't entirely recognize. His voice sounded calm on the surface, but a river of emotion ran underneath. "I won't," he said again.

Da spun around, both fists up in fighting position. Mick

stood in the cabin doorway, his temple pulsing as he waited for his father to make a move toward him.

The wind had scuttled the clouds away. Moonlight washed the clearing, which seemed to widen, then shrink. Every needle on the surrounding pines was clear, distinct. A night bird took wing, the slight wind through its feathers a whisper.

Da dropped his fists, but he took a step toward Mick, his face as dark as a thundercloud.

"I'm not going to the mining district up north," Mick said. "I'm going to Spokane to meet a friend of Mr. Delaney's. I'll work for his newspaper and save money for college."

His father measured him with his eyes, as if weighing Mick's worth on a scale.

"Now I've worked in a mine," Mick nodded at his da, "I have more respect for you and what you've done." He paused. Da just stood staring at him, so he went on. "But there's power in the written word, just as there is strength in a man's muscles. If I get an education—maybe become a newspaper reporter—I can do a lot to help the cause of the workingman."

Finally, Da shrugged and shook his head. "You're stubborn as your mam," he said. "Let's get moving. We'll lose two, three days going roundabout to Spokane." He started down the trail.

Mick turned back for a moment to blow out the flame in the cabin. A million stars lit the sky. He wouldn't need a miner's candle.

Author's Note

This story is fiction, but it is based on events that actually happened in the Coeur d'Alene Mining District in 1899. Mick Shea and his family are imaginary, but other characters in the book were real people who lived through the incidents described.

On April 29, 1899, a group of union miners climbed aboard a Northern Pacific train in Burke, Idaho. Threatening the engineer, Levi Hutton, with rifles, they ordered him to run the train down to Wardner, picking up more men and dynamite at mining camps along the way. Swarming with union men, many in disguise, the train pulled into Wardner Junction loaded with dynamite. Later it came to be called "the Dynamite Express." Meanwhile, Frederick Burbidge, manager of the Bunker Hill and Sullivan Mining Company, had received word of the growing mob, and he warned his non-union workers to look out for their safety. Shoshone County Sheriff James Young urged the crowd to disperse and go home, but it did not. Some men carried the dynamite to the nearby Bunker Hill ore-concentrating mill and set it off. A newspaper headline the next day read, "Bunker Hill Mill Blown off the Map by a Mob of Miners."

Idaho's Governor Frank Steunenberg wired President William McKinley, asking him to call out the military to suppress the insurrection in Shoshone County. Federal troops under Brigadier General Henry Clay Merriam arrived and arrested about a thousand men, locking them in a crude stockade. Most of the prisoners were union miners, but some were townspeople who sympathized with the union cause. Others were simply people who were in the wrong place at the wrong time.

Conner Malott was a reporter for the *Spokesman-Review,* one of the newspapers in the region that did not identify with the labor union movement. He wrote: "It was one of the most remarkable arrests ever made in any country. The captors recognized neither class nor occupation." At one point a local newspaper editor was thrown into the stockade and his printing press confiscated because his editorials criticized the treatment of the prisoners.

Some men managed to escape from the bullpen, as the stockade was known. A story is still told today about a woman who visited her husband in the stockade, bringing along their baby. She pinched the baby, who let out a loud cry, distracting the soldier on guard. Her husband was able to get away in the resulting commotion. Oral tradition in the Coeur d'Alenes also tells of weapons concealed in food and passed to inmates. Several prisoners did escape dressed in army uniforms, as described, and another group tried to dig their way out with spoons. They were caught before they could complete their tunnel.

Authorities gradually began to release some of the men in mid-May, admitting they were innocent. But close to one hundred and fifty remained in custody for up to six months without charges or legal recourse. Three men died while held prisoner in the bullpen. Prosecutors never presented enough evidence to convict anyone of murder, arson, or conspiracy in connection with the destruction of the Bunker Hill mill or the shooting death of a man that day. Thirteen men were tried in federal courts and convicted of the lesser charge of interfering with the U.S. mail, as the train hijacked during the incident happened to be carrying a mailbag. One man, Paul Corcoran, was convicted of second-degree murder in the shooting, but he was pardoned of the crime in 1901 and returned to the Coeur d'Alenes a hero to many.

As news filtered out of the Coeur d'Alenes, protests arose across the country, especially concerning the declaration of martial law and the inhumane conditions in the bullpen. The controversy eventually sparked congressional hearings, which ended when most politicians defended government action to keep the peace and protect the property of the mine owners.

In the wake of the explosion, mine owners in conjunction with state and federal authorities set up a "permit" hiring system that outlawed union workers. The character Godfrey Snipes is modeled after a real man who oversaw the so-called yellow-dog contract, which barred union members from the Coeur d'Alene mines for a generation. It was said that this man never forgot a face, forcing union miners to leave the district and find work elsewhere.

Within six months the Bunker Hill Company had constructed a new mill and restarted operations with non-union labor. Safety and fairness for workers came slowly. The government continually sided with business interests over labor until the 1930s. Mining remained the major industry in the Coeur d'Alenes for a century. Known today as the Idaho Silver Valley, the area is the richest proven silver mining district in the world. By 1985 mines in the valley had produced more than a billion ounces of silver. Today all but two mines have shut down due to lower silver prices, the cost of environmental protection, and cheaper operating and labor costs in South America and Africa.

In 1982 the U.S. Environmental Protection Agency (EPA) designated twenty-one square miles of the Silver Valley one of the largest and most dangerous pollution sites in the nation. For a century the byproducts of mining, including lead, zinc, mercury and other heavy metals, sat piled in heaps on the ground, washed down rivers and streams, and were dispersed through the air in the Coeur d'Alenes. The EPA declared that lead levels in the region threatened children's health; scientists have found heavy-metal contamination in every species of fish and wildlife studied in the area. Cleanup of the pollution has begun, but not without numerous court battles involving mining companies, the government, and the Coeur d'Alene Indian Tribe over how much cleanup is necessary and who should pay for it. The final bill could top one billion dollars.

Today, residents of the Coeur d'Alenes still place their hopes for the future in the natural riches of the region's mountains and valleys. But where they once bragged of the world's largest underground mine, the Bunker Hill, they now advertise outdoor recreation such as skiing, snowmobiling, mountain biking, backpacking, river rafting, canoeing, hunting, and fishing.